The Wicked Wife

Blackhaven Brides
Book 9

MARY LANCASTER

Books from Dragonblade Publishing

Dangerous Lords Series by Maggi Andersen
The Baron's Betrothal
Seducing the Earl
The Viscount's Widowed Lady

Also from Maggi Andersen
The Marquess Meets His Match

Knights of Honor Series by Alexa Aston
Word of Honor
Marked by Honor
Code of Honor
Journey to Honor
Heart of Honor
Bold in Honor
Love and Honor
Gift of Honor
Path to Honor

Legends of Love Series by Avril Borthiry
The Wishing Well
Isolated Hearts
Sentinel

The Lost Lords Series by Chasity Bowlin
The Lost Lord of Castle Black
The Vanishing of Lord Vale
The Missing Marquess of Althorn
The Resurrection of Lady Ramsleigh

By Elizabeth Ellen Carter
Captive of the Corsairs, *Heart of the Corsairs Series*
Revenge of the Corsairs, *Heart of the Corsairs Series*
Shadow of the Corsairs, *Heart of the Corsairs Series*
Dark Heart

Knight Everlasting Series by Cassidy Cayman
Endearing
Enchanted
Evermore

Midnight Meetings Series by Gina Conkle
Meet a Rogue at Midnight, book 4

Second Chance Series by Jessica Jefferson
Second Chance Marquess

Imperial Season Series by Mary Lancaster
Vienna Waltz
Vienna Woods
Vienna Dawn

Blackhaven Brides Series by Mary Lancaster
The Wicked Baron
The Wicked Lady
The Wicked Rebel
The Wicked Husband
The Wicked Marquis
The Wicked Governess
The Wicked Spy
The Wicked Gypsy
The Wicked Wife

Highland Loves Series by Melissa Limoges
My Reckless Love
My Steadfast Love
My Passionate Love

Clash of the Tartans Series by Anna Markland
Kilty Secrets
Kilted at the Altar
Kilty Pleasures

Queen of Thieves Series by Andy Peloquin
Child of the Night Guild
Thief of the Night Guild
Queen of the Night Guild

Table of Contents

Chapter One

FRANCES, COUNTESS OF Torridon, woke to discover her husband sitting on the edge of her bed. Her heart fluttered. She had almost forgotten how darkly handsome he was, how the smoke-grey of his hard eyes could ignite with lust.

She smiled. "What are you doing here?"

"Admiring the beauty of my sleeping wife." He leaned down to her and at the first touch of his lips, desire flared, hot and wonderful. She reached up and touched his cheek, but he lifted his head after a mere moment.

"Your son still sleeps," she said huskily.

He took her hand and kissed it, just a little too hard for civility. "I know. I have picked the wrong morning to depart."

"Depart?" She sat up. "Where are you going?"

"Just over to Ardnacraig, but I'll need to start now. I'll be back tomorrow afternoon."

"I'll come with you," she said brightly. Suddenly, she craved company more than anything in the world. Well, it wasn't really so sudden. The longing had been growing for weeks. Besides, she wanted to be with her husband. And to escape her mother-in-law for a day and a night seemed like bliss.

"I wish you could," he said ruefully. "But I have to leave now to get there by three as I promised. And we can't take Jamie."

"I don't see why not, and I can be ready in five minutes."

He smiled. "No, you can't. Besides, one of us should keep my mother company or she won't feel welcome."

She isn't.

Torridon released her hand and stood. The decision had been made before he entered the room and would not be altered.

"She's *your* mother," Frances snapped. "*You* stay and keep her company. Jamie and I shall visit Ardnacraig."

His smile became a little fixed. He did not like to quarrel with her. "If you feel competent to discuss the boundary drainage and related matters—"

"Of course I do," she interrupted. "I was born on an estate not so unlike this one. I knew as much about running it as my brother, before it was decreed my poor feminine brain could only handle subjects like dresses, balls, and babies."

"Frances—"

Encouraged by the gentleness of his tone, she said passionately, "I don't want to go without you, Alan. I want to go *with* you, and truthfully, there is no reason why I should not. I have had a baby, not a sickness, and neither of us are weak or ailing, whatever your mother says."

"Frances, she does know about these things," he replied in the familiar tone of patience she so hated. "She has had a few children of her own."

"But I am not her," Frances said, jumping out of bed. She caught his wrist as he would have walked away. "And Jamie is not any of her babies who died so sadly."

But she had lost him. She had never really had him. She saw that quite clearly in his cold, impatient eyes. "If you will not be guided by my mother, then please respect *my* wishes. Please stay here and look after my house, my mother, and my son. Those things are not nothing to me."

"Or to me!" She twined her fingers through his, stepped closer to him, desperate to make him understand. "Alan, I just want to be your wife again, not your burden or your nursery maid."

As soon as the words spilled out, she knew they were the wrong ones. But she could not take them back. His eyes almost froze over like the loch in winter.

Gently, yet deliberately, he disentangled their hands and stepped back. "I have given you no cause to imagine such things," he said coldly. "I have given you everything."

"Have you, Alan?" she whispered. "Have you really?"

He stared at her, his eyes unreadable, although she could have sworn that at last some storm raged beneath the ice. "What would you like now? Diamonds? Silk? A new carriage? Just speak to MacDonald and he will arrange it."

If he had slapped her it would have hurt less. Was that what he truly thought of her? After more than a year of marriage? That she was just some discontented, grasping female? The blood drained from her face so fast she had to seize the bedpost to steady herself.

He didn't notice, for he was already striding to the door. "Goodbye, Frances. I shall see you tomorrow afternoon."

The door closed behind him with a sharp click.

"How dare you?" she whispered. "How dare you even *think* such things! I have given you no cause to—"

Inevitably, Jamie began to cry in the next room. At almost four months old, James Ross, Viscount Inchkeith, was quite imperious when hungry. Fueled by anger with his father, Frances almost burst into the nursery and snatched the baby from his surprised nurse.

I have had enough. I won't let him oppress me like this. I will not be kept a prisoner in my own home. If I don't have his love, then I must have something or I'll die here...

She sat and began to feed Jamie, absently stroking his head as she thought. *No one dies from lack of love.*

No, well, he shall not order my life from his lack. I have family of my own. I have friends...

Ariadne Marshall. The most outrageous of her London friends was in Edinburgh, winding up her late husband's Scottish estate. If only she was still there...

Excitement surged, and with it formed a plan to escape, to enjoy a little of the fun she had been so starved of since before Jamie's birth.

And more than anything, she would show Torridon how wrong he was to behave like this.

AROUND DUSK THE following evening, Frances's coach, ablaze with the Torridon arms, came to a halt in Edinburgh's gracious Charlotte Square. Frances gazed down at the sleeping Jamie and wondered guiltily if she had made a terrible mistake. Not in coming away. Things could not go on as they were, and she was more than happy to show Torridon a little spirit. But perhaps Ariadne was not quite the right person to choose as her companion...

Frances remained inside the coach as the boy dismounted and stood at the horses' heads. Only then did the coachman himself dismount and make his stately way to Ariadne Marshall's front door. He gave it a sharp rap.

She is not at home, Frances thought in despair. Now she and Jamie would have to put up somewhere in Edinburgh until morning, and then word would inevitably get back to Torridon... the only question would be whether she should face his wrath at his home, or her family's. If she could outrun him. But if she did not stop for the night, if she simply changed horses in Edinburgh, they could drive through the night and be in Blackhaven by morning.

A cry from outside dragged her gaze back to Ariadne's front door just as Ariadne herself flew out of the gate and wrenched open the coach door.

"It *is* you!" she exclaimed. "Frances, how wonderful!" In her droll way, she peered into the dark corners of the carriage. "Where is he?"

"If you mean Torridon, I imagine he is at home," Frances said dryly. "If you mean my son, here he is."

Ariadne accorded the baby a cursory glance. "I don't do well with infants. They always cry at me. But you had best bring it in all the same!"

"So," Ariadne said, as they finally sat down to dinner alone together. The baby was asleep in the bedchamber hastily allotted to Frances, watched over by Ariadne's personal maid, Lawson, who had merely sniffed when given the instruction.

"You will fetch me if he wakes at all?" Frances had urged.

"Of course, my lady," Lawson had replied woodenly.

Frances met the gaze of her friend over the table, and lifted her fork. "So, what?"

"So, what brings you here?" Ariadne asked. "Have you quarreled with him?"

"What makes you think so?"

"I've met him. I'm surprised you could wait so long."

"Stop it, Ari, I won't traduce my husband with you. I only wanted a break, a little conversation, a little fun."

"How did you escape?"

"I simply ordered the coach, directed it to the village, and then south from there. Torridon keeps horses on all the roads he's likely to use. And I stayed last night at a very respectable inn."

"Then no one knows you are here?"

"They will when the coachman returns. And of course, I shall write to Torridon."

"Of course you will, though I can't think why."

Frances shrugged, as though she did not care. "He will be anxious for his son."

"If you're to have fun," Ariadne said, leaning over to pour wine into Frances's glass, "you should probably have left the child with his nurse."

"But I couldn't do that. I'm feeding him—much to my mother-in-law's annoyance. She had a wet-nurse picked out for him, and now claims that Jamie's feeding from me is the cause of my ill-health."

Ariadne glanced up uneasily from her plate. "Are you in ill-health?"

"Lord, no. I have a sneaking feeling old Lady Torridon knows it, too, but Torridon himself does not! I am in an impossible situation, for if I remonstrate or object to anything, it is immediately put down to the hysteria of a sick woman weakened by childbirth! As a result, I am hemmed in by an army of servants to care for Jamie and for me, all specially chosen for their sour faces by my devoted mother-in-law. And it's only got worse since my own mother's visit in January." She drew in a breath, even managed a bright smile. "But I shall not bore you with that. How are you, Ari? How are you bearing life without Tom?"

"Much as I bore life with him," Ariadne replied lightly. "I miss him, for no one ever called him dull. But I cannot say widowhood has changed my life much."

"It was such a shock. I was so sorry to hear of his death."

"Yes, I was grateful for your letter," Ariadne said, so casually that Frances knew she wanted the subject changed. Some wounds should not be poked.

"How goes your business in Edinburgh?" she asked instead.

Ariadne wrinkled her nose and finished chewing before she replied. "It's completed, but not terribly satisfactorily. I had hoped the Scottish estate would amount to something, even if only to pay off the debts of the English one, but apparently not. I've sold this house, of course—much to the annoyance of my sisters-in-law who have a fancy to live in it, but it is mine to do with as I choose, and I choose to live in London."

"I suppose it would be cheaper to live in Scotland," Frances suggested.

"Who wants to be cheap? I want to live the rest of my life with fun and adventure, without Tom's myriad relations popping out from behind pillars all over the world just to disapprove of me."

Frances laughed at the image, but with a sense of genuine sympathy. "I know what you mean. Wouldn't it be wonderful to be anonymous for a day? To do what we liked and have no one report us to disapproving family?"

"Go in disguise you mean?" Ariadne said with a sour smile. "Some hope. Family rarely needs to get reports. Some member or other is always there to recognize one."

"Oh, I don't know." Frances sipped her wine in fond reminiscence.

"Serena and I once dressed up in the maids' clothes, talked the local milliner into lending us hats, and went to an al fresco party on Blackhaven beach with all the fishermen and townspeople. No one recognized us. And we had grown up there."

"How old were you?"

"Fourteen. Maybe fifteen."

"They'd recognize you now," Ariadne said with certainty.

Frances followed the sudden spark of excitement. "Oh, I don't know about that. Let us experiment and see if we cannot fool your sisters-in-law."

"Disguised as a maid?" Ariadne asked, amused.

"Or a washerwoman or a beggar, whatever we can think of!"

"And what will you do? Watch from your elegant carriage?"

"No, for it will leave for Torridon tomorrow. I'll come with you to observe, of course."

Ariadne regarded her and then laughed. "Adventure it is, then, my dear. But if I am discovered, you must support me!"

They talked it over for a little longer, but after two days travelling over often poor roads, Frances was shattered. After dinner, Ariadne accompanied her to her bedchamber and relieved Lawson from her task. As though he smelled his own supper, Jamie promptly woke up.

"I shall feed the little brute and then retire," Frances said apologetically. "Tomorrow, I shall be more fun."

"Don't be silly. I'm so glad to have you. I'd have fled south from boredom tomorrow if you hadn't appeared at my door to save me. Feed your brute, and I shall unpack for you, since Lawson clearly considered the task beneath her dignity."

"You don't pay her to look after me," Frances excused. "Or Jamie."

"How much work does staring at a sleeping baby entail?" Ariadne wondered, opening the portmanteau. "You didn't bring much, did you? And most of this appears to belong to your hungry little beast... this is pretty, though."

Frances, sprawled on the bed and feeding Jamie, glanced up at the evening gown of deep blue embroidered in gold. "I've never worn it. I brought it on impulse, even though it probably doesn't fit me any longer."

Ariadne hung it up with her morning gown and put her few other garments and Jamie's into drawers. She was about to close the portmanteau when something else caught her eye, for she delved back in and came out with a jewel case.

Frances's heart bumped. "Oh no."

"What?" Ariadne asked, opening the case. Her eyes widened. "Oh my goodness," she said reverently. "Frances, these are beautiful!"

"The Torridon rubies," Frances said in annoyance. "Alan had them re-set for me as a wedding gift. They must have been in that wretched portmanteau since we first came to Scotland! Certainly, I have been nowhere that I could wear them since I arrived."

"Well, we must make sure you get a chance during your escape," Ariadne said comfortably. "For truly, it's a crime not to wear such exquisite jewels when you possess them."

"I should not be gallivanting with them! Do put them back in the portmanteau, Ari, so I don't forget them!"

Ariadne closed the case slowly and reluctantly. She wore an expression Frances had seen many times before, one that made her smile in anticipation. Instead of replacing the case in the portmanteau, Ariadne dropped it on the bed. "One moment!"

She rushed out of the room.

"What is she up to now?" Frances asked Jamie, who stopped feeding to smile at her and then carried on.

A minute later, Ariadne strode back into the room with another jewel case, which she set beside the rubies and opened. "My diamonds and your rubies."

Frances blinked. "What about them?"

"What do they look like to you?"

"Expensi—" Frances broke off, her breath catching as she met her friend's gaze. "They look like stakes in a wager. Only I can't wager the Torridon rubies. They're not mine, but part of the Torridon estate."

"Then you had better make sure you win. Or at least don't lose.

Let's see if I can fool Susan and Euphemia tomorrow, then we'll bolt down to Blackhaven the day after and see if you can fool your family. If you succeed and I don't, you get my diamonds. If *I* succeed and *you* don't, I get your rubies."

"Seriously, Ari, you can't have Torridon's rubies."

"Oh, don't be such an old stick! You can 'buy' them back from me or something. But I get to wear them for a night!"

"If you win," Frances taunted.

"Frances, no one is more recognizable than you. Of course I shall win."

WITH A LITTLE discreet use of Ariadne's face paint, Frances gave her friend a few extra lines of anxiety and some sleepless shadows under her eyes. Then she backcombed her hair until it stuck up at all sorts of odd angles and thrust in a couple of random pins to let the hair straggle down from them. Ari's last remaining footman was sent to scuff and rip her oldest pair of boots.

"All very well," Ariadne said, gazing at herself in the glass. "But where am I to get some horrible old clothes?"

"You only need one garment," Frances assured her. "Perhaps two, providing they cover all the rest." She drew a blanket off Ariadne's bed. "Well, you won't miss it for tonight, and I doubt you'll sleep here again."

"I planned to take the bedding with me."

"Not this one," Frances said cheerfully. When the footman came back with the badly scuffed boots, she thanked him in delight and handed him the blanket and a torn Paisley shawl that Ariadne had been about to throw away. "Do you think you could drag these through the garden? Get a good lot of mud—and even rubbish—on them. Oh, and maybe let the kitchen cat play with them for half an hour?"

The footman glanced rather wildly at Ariadne, who merely waved him away with amusement. He bowed and went to do their bidding.

Ariadne complained loudly when Frances tied the disgusting shawl half over her bizarre hair, and wrapped the blanket round her to cover her fine gown. She tied it around Ariadne's middle with a piece of string and stood back to admire her work.

"Though I say it myself, your own mother wouldn't know you," Frances said with satisfaction. "So what chance do mere sisters-in-law have?"

"You do realize you're talking yourself out of my diamonds? To say nothing of your own rubies."

"Torridon's rubies," Frances corrected somewhat mechanically.

"Though actually, you know, I do still look like me," Ariadne said uneasily. "I don't really want Susan and Euphemia to see me like this."

"They won't look. People of a certain class don't really see those beneath them without a very good reason. Could you describe to me the last washerwoman you saw? The last vagrant or even someone else's maid?"

"I take your point, Frannie, but how the devil do we get out of the house like this?"

Frances, having donned her smart pelisse, picked up Jamie and wrapped him in warm—clean—shawls. "We get your kind footman to smuggle you out. Pretending to *throw* you out would probably work best. And when I emerge from the front door, I'll follow you at a discreet distance to your sisters' house to observe."

The plan was duly followed. For a moment, Ariadne lingered at the top of the area steps while Frances, at the front gate, looked regally through her across the square. Ariadne complained that the footman had seemed to derive a little too much pleasure from pushing her out of the kitchen door. "I'd dismiss him," she finished, "if this was not his last day."

"You mean to stay here with no servants but Lawson?" Frances asked, surprised.

"And the cook. I told you, I would have fled to London this morn-ing had you not given me a reason to stay—at least until tomorrow, when we're off to Blackhaven."

In the light of day, Frances discovered she still liked that part of the plan. She had a yearning for home, for her own stern mother and her brother and sisters... she hadn't even met Serena's husband or Gervaise's wife. And she really wanted to see Serena before she went south to her husband's estate in Devon.

Her thought jolted back to reality as Ariadne, taking her role to heart, hobbled past the gate, bent almost double inside her bulky blanket. She even muttered at the gentleman walking up the road. He glared at her as if she had no right to be in such a hallowed neighborhood. Ariadne cackled, and Frances had to smother her laughter as she closed the gate and followed her friend to the end of the square and further into Edinburgh's gracious new town.

Ariadne waddled past most people at a good pace. Her sisters-in-law apparently kept to a strict routine, and she was anxious to catch them as they left home on their way to perform charitable work at the church. Otherwise, there would be a lot of dull waiting around. However, two thin, middle-aged women strode energetically uphill toward them, and Ariadne glanced back over her shoulder. These unfashionably dressed ladies must be their quarry.

"Good morning, ladies," Ariadne addressed them in an impressively strong Edinburgh accent. "Spare a poor old woman a penny on such a beautiful day?"

The sky was gray and beginning to drizzle, but this didn't seem to be what offended the Marshall ladies. "Outrageous! Begging in the street!" one exclaimed, grasping the arm of the other and trying to hurry past.

"Please, ma'am, it's for the children..."

"I'll have you taken up," one of the ladies threatened. "You and your children!" And they sailed on, leaving Ariadne staring after them with theatrical fury.

Trying not to laugh, Frances passed them with the faintest nod of acknowledgement, which they barely returned. Their ill-nature seemed to have no basis in class.

Frances took a sovereign from her reticule and pressed it into Ariadne's too-soft hand. "For your children," she said loudly. "Make them a good broth."

"I'm more likely to make them *into* broth," Ariadne said below her breath. Then more loudly, "Thank you kindly, ma'am. God bless you!"

They turned the next corner together, and Ariadne straightened, tearing off the blanket. "This thing stinks! What on earth did George do with it?"

"Let's not ask," Frances said, smiling at a baffled family who were passing them. "After all, it served its purpose. They most certainly did not recognize you."

"Well, you can't have my diamonds yet. Let us hire a chaise to Blackhaven."

Chapter Two

ALAN ROSS, EARL of Torridon, had left Ardnacraig at dawn despite the inevitable conviviality of the night before. Although still angry with his wife for her several attacks during their quarrel, he recognized he had been both unkind and unfair in imputing greed to her. She had never asked him for anything—except to come with him to Ardnacraig—and he knew in his heart her insults had come from unhappiness, not ill-nature.

Guilt for that unhappiness ate at him. She either could not see or did not care that he was taking care of her. It was not enough for her. It broke his heart that even though she had given him a son, he could not make her happy. Of course, she had been pleasing her family in accepting his offer, but he had once had reason to hope there was more to their relationship than convenience and family alliance.

Even yesterday morning when he had wakened her, her eyes had been soft and welcoming, her voice husky with desire as she told him their son still slept. It had taken extraordinary self-denial not to ravish her where she lay, but his mother had told him he must not touch his wife in that way for at least six months after the birth, not until her body was fully healed.

It appalled him now that Frances might have offered herself through boredom, as a means of persuading him to let her see other people, and if things were as wrong as that, then he was responsible and needed to try to make them right. And so, he left Ardnacraig several hours before he'd meant to, and rode hard through the glen to Torridon House, with every intention of spending the afternoon with his wife doing whatever she wished to do. And talking over what would make her happier. Providing it did not compromise her safety or Jamie's, he would move heaven and earth to give it to her.

His heart beat faster as he finally rode up to the house. In truth, his wish to see her was not unselfish. It never had been. And now that she had forced him to see her isolation from her point of view, he thought they could compromise and be better friends once more. In the two months left of his self-imposed abstinence, he would court her all over again, worship her, tame her wicked tongue, win her...

He threw himself from the horse, his body hot with a longing he would not indulge, and yet there was excitement in that, too...

"Drummond," he said, spotting his butler as he all but threw his overcoat and hat at the footman, and strode across the hall to the stairs. "Where is her ladyship?"

"Her ladyship has not yet come home, my lord. The dowager countess is in the morning room."

Torridon paused, frowning. "Not come home? Where did she go?"

"Into the village, sir, with his wee lordship. Gordon took her in the coach."

Despite his disappointment, Torridon had to hide a smile. She was paying him back. Still, it gave him time to wash the mud and sweat from his body and change his clothes.

Two hours later, she still had not come home, and Torridon began to think of his afternoon as wasted. Perhaps this was how Frances regarded all her afternoons... although she had the baby to care for in ways he could not. It was she who had insisted on feeding Jamie herself, instead of employing the wet nurse his mother had recommended.

The trouble was, he had so many things to do on the estate, for he was learning as he went. He was never meant to have been the earl, and had known nothing of land management when his brother Andrew had died so unexpectedly. Alan was a soldier, conscientiously learning a new "trade" for which he was ill-suited.

"Did she not say when she would be back?" Torridon demanded of his mother as he stared out the window at the teeming rain.

"She didn't say anything at all," his mother said tartly. "At least, not to me. She left without troubling to say goodbye."

Torridon frowned. "Well, she isn't obliged to report her outings to you. You certainly don't report yours to her." He flung himself away from the window, heading for the door. "I'm going to meet her."

"In this downpour?" his mother demanded, affronted.

"In this downpour," he agreed over his shoulder.

"Alan, don't be angry with her," his mother called after him. "She does not mean to be so selfish. In fact, I'm sure she does not wish to drag you out in such weather..."

Her words followed him across the hall, setting up his hackles because they sounded more like criticism than defense. No wonder Frances had not cared to be left to keep his mother's company if she was in this kind of mood.

Demanding a fresh horse be saddled immediately, he struggled into a dry greatcoat.

"OH AYE, I saw the carriage go by," Mrs. MacSorley at the village shop told him. "But it didn't stop."

Torridon scowled, unease beginning to tug at him, but he remembered to thank Mrs. MacSorley before leaving the shop and remounting. On this road, within visiting distance, there was really only the church and the manse. He supposed she might have gone to the church and then been buttonholed by the minister's wife, who was not really a great friend of hers. He rode in that direction and eventually discovered the minister about to take tea with his family. Mr. MacDonald welcomed him with delight and bade him join them.

"Thank you, no, I'm looking for my wife. Mrs. MacSorley thought she came this way, and I wondered if she had called on you?"

"Oh no," Mrs. MacDonald said, her eyes widening, no doubt with a special thrill at the possibility of juicy gossip from the big house.

"I saw the coach," one of the children piped up, "driving away from the village. Pulled by two beautifully matching black—"

"Ah, thank you," Torridon interrupted hurriedly. "I must have misunderstood her. Sorry to interrupt you, ma'am! I'll leave you to your tea."

Escaping, Torridon threw himself back onto the horse and galloped for home. A terrible suspicion had begun to form in his mind. Now that he really thought about their last encounter, was his wife's behavior not that of a woman at the end of her tether? He might not understand how or why, but he had known of her unhappiness and done nothing about it, preferring to wait patiently until the old Frances reemerged.

Shame on you, Ross. Although he had been the earl for over a year, he still thought of himself as Captain Ross rather than Lord Torridon. *Shame on you for being a selfish, stupid monster of a man...*

Even so, he could not help hoping he was wrong, and that he would find her already returned and waiting for him. And this time, *this* time, he would lay his heart at her feet, as he should always have done instead of... whatever it was he had done and hadn't done. He would worry about such details later. Of the first importance was her safety and their son's.

But she had not come home. Barging into her chamber, still dripping from his hair and boots, he rang for her maid, and threw open cupboards and drawers. But he could not tell what was missing, not from her things or from Jamie's in the nursery. When Carter, the maid, arrived, he commanded her to look.

He must have been scowling ferociously, for she all but cowered as she passed him.

"The small portmanteau is gone," Carter reported in a shaken voice. "Also, her ladyship's brown travelling dress, the peach day dress, and the new blue evening gown. Some undergarments. Her walking boots and a pair of evening slippers."

Torridon swung away to the window and closed his eyes. "And jewelry?"

The maid opened another drawer. "No, there is nothing gone... oh." She scratched around a little more until he swung impatiently back to her. "The rubies," she blurted. "The rubies are gone."

He had never felt, never expected such fierce pain, such emptiness. Almost like when his brother had died, or when his comrades had been killed in Spain...

But she was not dead. He would not grieve. She had run away from him, taking the rubies that he had given her, to pawn, perhaps, or to keep herself. More than that, much more, she had put herself and their son in danger, and he could never forgive that.

In the meantime, she'd also put him in the damnably difficult position of saving her honor. The scandal of her flight would be instant, and as soon as she tried to pawn the rubies, the stones would be recognized and then...

"Her ladyship has gone earlier than planned to visit her family in Blackhaven," he barked at the maid. "She wants to see her sister before she departs for Devon." He turned and glared at Carter. "And if you even hint at anything different, you'll be dismissed without a character. Do you understand?"

"Yes, sir, yes, my lord," Carter stammered, curtseying several times, as if she didn't know what else to do.

Torridon, who could not abide people who were afraid of him, stormed out of the room in disgust and went to prepare for his own departure.

NOT FOR AN instant did Torridon himself vary from the tale he had given the maid. For one thing, once he thought about it more calmly, he was pretty sure it was true. For another, he couldn't bear the speculation of his affronted parent. He told her he had found word in his wife's chamber, which was true enough in its own way. Then he retired early to bed, and in the morning, set off in his travelling coach, taking with him his valet and a trunk containing his own clothes and several more of his wife's.

After some thought, he did not take Carter or the nursery maid with him. If Frances had valued either servant, she would have taken them with her. Even through his hurt and fury, he recognized that fact and the likelihood that she was correct in her judgment. Either that, or she was shrugging off everything connected to him—apart from his son.

Pausing for dinner at the usual inn, The Rampant Lion, he learned that Frances had indeed spent last night there. It was a relief, but it also called out the hunter in him. He was on her trail. And being still with Gordon the coachman and his boy, she was as safe as anyone could be on the road. He would have pressed on through the night in the hope of catching her, except that Frances had taken his horses, and the spare animals The Rampant Lion had to offer didn't seem to be up to much. He decided he would be quicker and kinder to let his own horses rest for the night and re-harness them in the morning.

The roads were easier on the following day. But as they came to the crossroads—straight on for Carlisle and the south, or east to Edinburgh—he leaned forward on impulse and rapped on the roof for the driver to halt.

Only about a week ago, she had mentioned Mrs. Marshall being in Edinburgh to sell her husband's house. Torridon hadn't paid much attention, for he didn't care for the brash widow. He enjoyed flirtation as much as the next man, but not after his engagement and certainly not with the friend of his betrothed. In his opinion, she was fast and grasping and quite untrustworthy, and he could not like Frances's friendship with her.

And Frances knew that. Frances was angry with him.

Making the detour to Edinburgh would add at least a day to his journey to Blackhaven. But if she was there…

He opened the window and gave the instruction.

NO ONE HE spoke to in Edinburgh seemed to find it odd that a gentleman should be asking for Mrs. Marshall's house when it was close to midnight. When he eventually found his way to Charlotte Square, there was a light in the kitchen but not in the main part of the house. He wondered if they had all retired to bed, or if, as seemed more likely, Frances was out with her friend at some party. If the latter, he hoped grimly they had left Jamie with proper care. By God, if they had not…

He rapped sharply on the door and rang the bell. When no one answered, he did both again rather more impatiently. Eventually, a faint light flickered in the arched window over the front door, and a moment later, he heard the bolts being pulled back.

A half-dressed footman stuck his bedraggled head and shoulders around the door. A woman stood poised behind him with a large candlestick raised like a weapon.

"Is Mrs. Marshall at home?" he snapped.

The man blinked. "No, sir. She's gone."

"Gone where?"

"Why would she tell me? I'm dismissed like everyone else. The house is sold."

"Take a guess," Torridon said unpleasantly.

"South," the footman blurted. "London, probably."

"Did she have companions?"

"Lady Torridon and the baby, sir. And Lawson, Mrs. Marshall's maid."

"In her ladyship's coach?"

"Oh, no, sir. A hired chaise called for them at five o'clock. With postilions and everything."

Relief washed over Torridon. They were safe. Whether they were heading to Blackhaven or London, they were safe.

"Are you Lord Torridon?" the footman asked reluctantly, probably because the woman with the candlestick was nudging him so forcefully.

"I am. Why?"

"Her ladyship left a letter for you. I was to post it in the morning, but since you're here…"

Torridon held out his hand and the woman, who had dashed off as soon as the footman began to speak, arrived back in time to place a sealed missive between his fingers. He broke it open and snatched the footman's candle in order to improve the light from the square.

My dear Torridon, she began. Not *my dear Alan*, as her letters had used to open. He felt the distance between them like a spear through his heart. *I hope you are not anxious, for I assure you there is no cause. I sent Gordon back to Torridon with the coach and a letter which you should have had by now. However, I have changed my mind and am no longer in Edinburgh, having a fancy instead to visit my sister in Devon. Jamie loves traveling; I think he likes the bumps and the shaking that everyone else hates!*

Hoping you are well and assuring you of our best, Frances.

Torridon crumpled the letter into a ball and thrust the candle back into the footman's surprised fingers. Without a word, he ran down the steps and out the gate, more furious than he had been since this silly escapade began. He was not fooled for a moment. She was not going all the way to Devon. She was trying to make him give up on any ideas he might have had of following her to Blackhaven.

The knowledge enraged him. For whatever his own folly and unconscious unkindness, he did not deserve such treatment. And he had had enough.

FRANCES FOUND HERSELF smiling as they drove into the town of Blackhaven. This town, and Braithwaite Castle on the hill, were home as Torridon could never be. Every street, every other building, held a memory of one kind or another, places she had played or quarreled with Serena, taken tea with friends, or bolted from in some childish mischief. Where she had walked arm-in-arm with Torridon, a year ago…

The last memory brought a lump to her throat before she could banish it. Newly married, she had been so happy, so full of hope for their future together, so blindly in love with the sternly handsome Scottish earl with his sardonic sense of humor and his tender kisses... Then she remembered that he had left Blackhaven the following day, having received word of his mother's sickness. And Frances had attended the annual spring ball at the castle alone.

Well, hardly alone, she thought, laughing at herself. She had been with her family and friends whom she'd known since childhood, and with new friends who had accompanied them from London.

"Oh my goodness," she said aloud, gazing at Ariadne. "This is the week of the spring ball, Blackhaven will be full of people we know."

"They won't count," Ariadne said. "You have to fool a sister. Or sister-in-law at the very least."

"I've never *met* my sister-in-law," Frances objected. "Or my brother-in-law. And an actual sister is a much harder proposition, especially if they know I'm here."

"Then pull down the veil on that ridiculous garb and leave me to do the talking," Ariadne instructed as the chaise pulled up at the imposing Blackhaven Hotel.

The ridiculous garb was, in fact, Ariadne's own black widow's weeds, bought to mourn her late husband, but rarely worn. Frances didn't actually like wearing them. For one thing, it felt like tempting providence with Torridon's life. For another, it crept into her head that the dress symbolized the end of her marriage, at least in any way that mattered to her. Sweeping such thoughts aside, she drew down the veil, clutched Jamie tighter, and alighted.

While the hotel porter took in their luggage, Lawson held the baby, and Frances paid off the post boys. Ariadne, meanwhile, sailed inside to arrange accommodation. Following her friend into the familiar, large foyer, Frances saw that she had forgotten her role already. They had decided that Frances should be the widow with an excuse to wear the veil where she was likely to know people, and Ariadne should be her submissive companion—about as unlike Ari's character as one could get. "Submissive" did not come easily or naturally to Ariadne Marshall. Frances would have to coach her before they ran into anyone likely to recognize them.

As they followed the boy upstairs to their rooms, it struck Frances that this jest was taking on a whole life of its own. And yet, it was only to be until she managed to run into some member of her family and prove they did not recognize her. They were staying at the hotel under assumed names—Mrs. Alan and Mrs. Thom—with complicated roles and pasts all mapped out. Frances had devised most of this because she really had to win the wager. The very thought of Ariadne having the rubies, even wearing them for one night, churned her stomach. Torridon would not see the joke, and Frances knew she was wrong to have ever indulged in the silly wager.

Still, there was something quite liberating in being someone else.

Ariadne had engaged a suite of rooms with a sitting room, two large bedchambers, and a tiny one for Lawson. Two hotel servants brought in a cradle for Jamie, which was placed in Frances's chamber.

It was very comfortable, almost luxurious, and Frances began to wonder for the first time how she was going to pay for it. She had only pin-money with her, which she doubted would stretch to these rooms, even for a mere couple of nights. She didn't really want to have the bill sent to Torridon. Well, perhaps she would win Ariadne's diamonds, sell them, and give poor Ari what was left after the bill was paid. After all, she suspected Ariadne had very little to live on. Tom Marshall, a reckless gambler and adventurer, had not left her with much.

"But this is charming!" Ariadne enthused. "We shall dine in style tonight in that very ornate restaurant we saw from the foyer—"

"We can't," Frances told her flatly. "Even if it's quiet and we know none of the guests, most of the hotel staff are Blackhaven people and are bound to know me. I can't eat with my veil on."

Ariadne's shoulders drooped.

"We can do so once this is over," Frances said hastily. "As soon as I have spoken to one sister or brother who does not recognize me, we can throw off our cover." She frowned. "Although perhaps we should stay at the castle after we do so, for it will be embarrassing to admit our false names to the hotel!"

Ariadne laughed. "Fine. Then let us have tea in our rooms, then sally forth and you may show me your town."

"GOODNESS," ARIADNE COMMENTED an hour or so later as they stood at the harbor. She gazed not out to sea, but along the shore to Braithwaite Castle perched on the cliff above the town. "It could have been drawn straight from knightly tales of old. Or from Mrs. Radcliffe. Does your family really live there?"

"Oh, yes, but it isn't all medieval stone turrets. Most of the old castle is in ruins, except for the bit Serena insisted on living in as soon as she escaped the nursery. There is a newer house built on to it, which makes much more comfortable living for the rest of us." She smiled and walked on toward the market, where the stalls were beginning to close. "When our wager is done, we could go to the ball, if you like."

Ariadne took her arm. "Apparently, it is a masked ball."

"Masked?" Frances exclaimed, startled. She laughed. "I wonder how Serena got that past my mother?"

"I believe it has become a craze in Blackhaven after some masked assembly ball."

Frances regarded her with fascination. "How do you know these things?"

"I ask and listen. How do you *not* know them? Doesn't your family write to you?"

"Yes, but I had already told them I could not come for this."

"Why not?" Ariadne demanded.

"My health. Torridon was afraid I was not recovering well from the birth."

"And yet, here you are, without even one pampering servant to look after you."

"You must not discount Lawson," Frances protested. "Who is even now looking after my... Gillie!"

Ariadne seized her arm as Frances instinctively veered across the market square toward the old friend she had just spotted strolling toward the harbor on her husband's arm. They made a handsome couple. Marriage and being a baroness appeared to suit Gillie very well.

"Lord Wickenden," Ariadne all but purred, although she pulled Frances onward.

"Behave," Frances warned her, resisting the urge to peer over her shoulder. "He is a married man and has just become a father. You know, Gillie lived here all her life, too. She even shared a governess with Serena and me for a year or two. She is almost a sister. Could I not just go and bump into her, and apologize and see if she knows me?"

"No," Ariadne said firmly. "She is not a sister."

"Susan and Effie are not your sisters, either," Frances pointed out.

"No, but that advantage is cancelled out by the fact that they knew I was in Edinburgh. That is a disadvantage *you* do not have here."

"I want to talk to Gillie and see her baby," Frances said ruefully.

"Then hurry up and find your sisters! Or your mother."

"My mother would boil me in oil for this escapade."

"Fun, isn't it?" Ariadne said, and Frances laughed, because truthfully, it was.

They were returning to the hotel via the quieter streets when Frances actually did glimpse one of her sisters. She began to smile behind her veil, gladness at the coming reunion vying with mischief as she wondered how far she could fool Maria. She was about to nudge Ariadne in warning when her sister turned her face up to her companion and smiled adoringly.

Startled—for she still thought of Maria as a child although she was now sixteen years old—Frances regarded the companion. A very young officer of the 44th who were barracked at Blackhaven, he was not known to Frances at all. Most of the regiment had joined Wellington in the Peninsula last year, so this man was probably a new recruit.

And something in his manner set Frances's back up. It wasn't simply that he seemed too familiar with Maria. After all, several officers were well known to all the best families in the area, including her own. But this man looked somehow… furtive.

All this, she gathered in an instant. A moment later, Maria flitted off in the direction of the church and the officer strode on.

And so, Frances said nothing about Maria to Ariadne. It was a trivial incident, for of course her sisters would have friends now that she did not know. But she could not shake off the anxiety that Maria was indulging in a clandestine and therefore dangerous assignation.

LORD TORRIDON, HAVING driven through the night, arrived at Braithwaite Castle before anyone but the servants were up. Paton, the butler, showed him into the breakfast room, where he availed himself of coffee and a vast plate of ham, eggs, cheese, and toast.

He was just tucking in when a young man wandered into the room. His rumpled dark hair was too long to be fashionable and his clothes were hardly the first stare of fashion.

Torridon, who never judged a man by appearance, nodded to him. "Good morning."

The newcomer paused in mid-yawn, eyebrows raised. "Oh! Good morning! I beg your pardon, I didn't know anyone was up yet." He strolled over and offered his hand with careless friendliness. "I'm Tamar."

"Are you, by God?" He regarded the man with more interest. The almost legendary and penniless lost marquis was rumored to be an excellent artist, among other eccentric things, and the polite world was not quite sure why the Earl of Braithwaite had permitted him to marry Lady Serena. "I'm Torridon."

Tamar blinked. "Frances's husband? How famous! Very glad to make your acquaintance at last. Serena will be delighted. She was quite cast down that you were not coming to the ball."

Torridon merely smiled. He had been too proud to ask Paton if his wife was there, and the same vice held him back from asking Lord Tamar. However, his agony was soon at an end because his brother-in-law, Lord Braithwaite, walked in a moment later, saying, "The whole place will be in uproar today, Tamar, so I suggest—good God."

Torridon rose to shake hands. "Alas, only me, and I hope you don't mind my consuming your breakfast."

Braithwaite laughed. "As long as you leave me a sliver of ham. I'm very glad to see you here! Where have you put Frances?"

Torridon's stomach gave a sickening lurch. He sat back down too quickly. Uncaring now for Tamar's presence—the whole story would be around the castle in no time, anyhow—he said, "She is not here, I take it. I was sure she was coming here. And Serena... the Tamars have not left for Devon."

"We're going after the ball," Tamar said, mystified. "Does this matter?"

"Have you lost Frances?" Braithwaite asked carefully, sitting beside him.

Torridon tried to smile. "In more ways than one. I followed her to Edinburgh where she stayed a night with Ariadne Marshall. They left together in a hired chaise..." He refocused his gaze on Braithwaite. "Might I trouble you for horses? Mine are done in, and I had better set off as soon as I've eaten."

"Hold on there, Torridon, don't go off half-cocked! Tell me what's happened."

Torridon, holding himself rigid, gave a brief account of the quarrel and his wife's sudden bolt. "Her letter said she was going to Devon. I thought she was trying to deter me from following her here, but perhaps it was the truth and she didn't know Serena was still in Blackhaven."

"I'll bet she knows," Braithwaite said shrewdly. "Besides, my mother and the girls are here, too, and I doubt she would pass up the chance to meet my wife. What's more, if the baby is with her, I can't see her travelling another four hundred miles. I expect you passed her on the road."

Torridon rubbed his forehead. He was too tired to think straight. "She could have stayed at any inn on the way," he allowed. "I should wait a little, shouldn't I?"

"Definitely." Braithwaite hesitated, then. "You know, she is subject to wild starts, but it is never from ill-nature."

"I know. I suppose I am more worried because of the company she is in."

"Ariadne Marshall? She is a little on the fast side, and Marshall was a bit of a loose screw, but I never heard anything terrible about her."

"I think she is little more than an adventuress," Torridon said bluntly. "I never forbade the friendship, but I cannot like her, and I don't see why Frances does."

"I expect the lady appeals to her wilder streak," Braithwaite said. "But Frances is not *weak*, Torridon. No one can make her do what she does not wish to."

Except you, when you made her marry me. Even as the thought entered his head, he knew it was not true. There was no coercion. Frances had been perfectly willing to marry him. He had believed she loved him. And, God help him, though he was a not a man who loved easily, she had enchanted him from the day he'd met her. But her nature was mercurial, and he knew those months spent at Torridon had begun to irk her. It hurt, but it could not change his own feeling.

Braithwaite gripped his shoulder. "You look exhausted. Get some sleep, and I shall make a few discreet enquiries. It won't do for you to barge all over town asking for sightings of your own wife!"

Chapter Three

STILL HEAVILY VEILED, Frances promenaded up and down the high street with Ariadne. Since it was the day before the spring ball, Frances knew that Serena would venture into the town at some point for last minute fripperies, or just to escape the massive, organized chaos of the preparations at the castle. Of course, these would now be the responsibility of the new countess, Gervaise's wife, but she doubted her mother would relinquish her hold on things very easily.

For the first time, it struck Frances that Lady Torridon was not so different from her own mother, which gave her pause… and a certain rueful sympathy for Gervaise's wife. He had not even married someone used to running a great house, but merely the lost heiress to Haven Hall who, according to Serena, had had quite an unconventional upbringing.

After two hours of gazing in shop windows and wandering around the art gallery while keeping watch on the street, Frances said, "I need to go back and feed Jamie. You must lunch in the restaurant and send me word if you glimpse Serena or Braithwaite."

"Very well. I wish we had put a time limit on this wager," Ariadne said. "If we had, I would already have won. It was much easier to find Susan and Effie in a city far larger than this."

"You knew where they lived and when they would leave the house," Frances pointed out. "We can hardly go and skulk at the castle gates and hope to be unnoticed!"

"Fair point," Ariadne allowed. "But if I have to look in that dress shop window one more time without buying anything—"

If she finished her sentence, Frances didn't hear it, for a sudden peel of quite recognizable laughter rang out on the other side of the street. It made her smile and jerk around at the same time, for the laugh could only belong to her youngest sister, Helen. And there, gazing in the shop window were the unmistakable figures of all her sisters.

Helen was pointing out a hat with great delight. "Oh, but you must have that one, Serena; it will be so funny!"

Frances began to cross the road, narrowly avoiding a cart which splattered mud on her skirts.

"Hush, child," Serena said tolerantly, "it is not my ambition to become a figure of fun in my new home. It is ribbon I need, not hats."

Frances snatched the handkerchief from Ariadne's hands as her sisters began to move away from the hat shop. Since Ari had been using it to disguise her face from Serena, who had met her more than once, she immediately turned her head aside as though gazing in the shop window.

Frances pursued her sisters. "Excuse me," she said in a husky voice with a very soft, Highland accent. "Did you drop this, young ladies?"

Inevitably, all four of them stopped and turned to face her. Her heart soared because they all looked so well and happy, and suddenly she wanted to cry. Serena was radiant, and the children so much more grown up than when she had seen them last. Especially Maria, who no longer looked like a child at all. She had become a very pretty young lady.

Holding out Ariadne's handkerchief, Frances tottered the last few steps toward them as though she were a much older woman. The thickness of the veil, she knew, would hide her features well enough.

"It was on the ground by the window," she said breathlessly.

"Oh, no, it isn't ours," Serena said after a quick, quizzical glance at each of the girls. "But thank you so much for asking."

Frances inclined her head and tottered back to Ariadne. "Perhaps it is yours?" she suggested.

"I expect it is." Ariadne snatched it back. "And... they've walked on. They didn't know you in the least. Drat you, Frannie, now we have a draw."

"So, we each keep our own jewels…"

"Oh no, such a dull end to our wager doesn't suit me at all! Or you. Come up with another plan."

"Hmm…."

"Well?" Ariadne pursued, immediately intrigued.

Frances watched her sisters continue to walk away from her, then turn into the new draper's shop. "We *could* go to the ball and see if anyone recognizes either of us. But we're only playing for honor now."

"And one night in each other's jewels."

Frances laughed. "You think you have me because this is my home and my family."

"Oh, I think it's more even than that. We'll both be masked. At a ball, you can avoid your family easily enough if you choose to, and there will be many people there, will there not, who know both of us?"

Laughter bubbled up again. It was good to be home. She took Ariadne's arm, drawing her on toward the hotel. Only then did she notice the young officer in red pausing outside the draper's shop to look at the tiny window display. She was sure it was the same officer she had seen with Maria yesterday.

ARIADNE'S ONE CONCESSION to discretion was to dress more quietly than usual, so as not to draw attention to herself. From experience, she knew she was quite adept at this when necessary. Leaving Frances bouncing the baby on her knee and making silly noises at him, she sallied forth into the late afternoon sunshine to look for masks for the ball and to see what other entertainment could be extracted from this provincial little town.

On her way across the hotel foyer, she noticed a great deal of activity in a room at the back, with tables and chairs being carried in and scraped across the floor, cloths being spread, and voices calling orders and acknowledgements.

"Is there a party tonight?" she asked the doorman while he held the door for her.

"A private club, ma'am. Gaming," he said in a disapproving voice. "Not frequented by *ladies*."

"Ah, I see. Thank you." She passed on with a gracious smile, hiding her rising excitement. A gaming club not frequented by ladies sounded ideal for her purpose.

In a ridiculously tiny draper's shop, she discovered a fine selection of masks, and asked the proprietor to put some aside for her friend to view later. Then she walked on to the market, which, however, was once more just finishing for the day. Beyond it was the pretty harbor, and she was just about to walk there when she spotted him.

Alan Ross, Earl of Torridon.

Her heart thundered. It always did at the sight of him. She didn't know why. He barely knew she existed. And the one time she'd forced him to acknowledge her, he had looked at her as though she were the dirt beneath his feet.

Of course, she had played her hand badly. She'd known he would never touch his wife's friend after they were married, so in desperation, she had attempted to seduce him while they were merely engaged.

He was no angel. She knew that because she'd made it her business to find out, but she'd waited too long for him to notice her without help, and suddenly, he was engaged to Frances of all people. More than that, the word was, he'd already broken off all contact with a string of disconsolate opera dancers and a beautiful married lady of the ton. Frances had been unaware these women existed. Ariadne had rather liked his honor in disconnecting himself from them... and made her play.

She had only wanted one night. She wouldn't even have taken anything from him. But she should have known his honor was not only for the world to admire. He lumped even one discreet night with her along with his infamous string of affairs and rejected her with unnecessary contempt. She couldn't forgive that. And yet seeing him now, striding past the market toward the harbor, her heart leapt and she wanted him still.

Frances did not know what to do with such a man. She didn't understand him. Ariadne wasn't sure she did either, but by God, she would know how to please him if she ever made it into his bed.

Frances had assumed he would not leave Torridon. Ariadne had expected him to be half way to Devon by now. Both, it seemed, had underestimated him. He'd found them out. But not yet *found* them.

Ideal. He would be at the ball, and he would know his wife immediately. Frances always paid up. The rubies would be in Ariadne's hands for one night. And one night was all she needed.

IN ASSUMING TORRIDON hadn't seen her, Ariadne was quite wrong. He had noticed her long before she caught sight of him. But he'd seen right away that Frances wasn't with her and he had no desire to speak to the woman he suspected of leading his wife astray. Instead, he looked straight ahead and walked past her to the harbor, where he waited for her to become bored with the view. And then, when she turned back toward the high street, he followed her.

There was no real thought behind his actions at this point, just disbelief and anger. For Mrs. Marshall did not look like a woman who had just arrived in a strange place. She knew her way. She had been here at least as long as he, and his wife with her. This went beyond everything else. This was deliberate deceit. His sweet, charming, wonderful wife was deceiving him. How or why, he did not know. Not that he truly suspected another man—for one thing, she had had little opportunity of meeting one in recent months—but that she had not gone to her family who lived less than two miles from the town... it staggered him. And made him fear for his child.

Without even glancing over her shoulder, Mrs. Marshall walked into the hotel. Following, Torridon was in time to see a hotel flunky bowing to her at the foot of the stairs. "Good afternoon, Mrs. Thom."

Her manner had changed, almost beyond recognition. "Oh my," she fluttered. "Good afternoon…" and she rushed upstairs as though she had just remembered something or was late for an appointment. There was very little sign of the supremely confidant, sophisticated woman Torridon knew.

And she was using a false name. Mrs. Thom. Thomas, or Tom, had been her husband's name.

Torridon sat down in one of the sofas with his back to the stairs, as though he were waiting for someone. In reality, his mind felt dull, almost blank with disappointment. Pain twisted through his gut.

On sudden impulse, he got up and went to the desk. "Which room is Mrs. Alan in?"

The clerk looked haughty, but only for an instant. Torridon gave him the stare which had reduced to jelly even the most self-important of subalterns.

"The west suite sir, on the far left of the first-floor hallway," the clerk gibbered, then looked to right and left to make sure, no doubt, that no one else had heard him break the hotel's policy.

Torridon laid some random money on the desk and set off purposely up the stairs. The passage was empty as he made his way along to the end door, where he hesitated. This was a suite of rooms, not just a bedchamber, so it was more than likely Mrs. Marshall lived there, too. Besides, he had no idea what he wished to say to his wife, even if she were alone. He only wanted to know that his son was safe.

But it was his wife's voice he heard first, loving and indulgent. "Are you not the cleverest baby ever? Catch the pretty ribbon."

And then came a happy, unmistakable gurgle.

Relieved beyond belief, he rested his forehead against the door. How could he feel this and so much anger and hurt at the same time?

In a more normal voice, Frances said, "Did you see anyone from the castle when you were out?"

"Not a soul," Mrs. Marshall said cheerfully. "To my knowledge, that is."

Which was interesting, because there had been a moment as he strode past the market that he was sure she had raised her head. Had she truly not seen him, then? And if she had, why would she not tell Frances?

"Control your impatience, Frannie," she drawled. "You'll see your family tomorrow night."

Torridon turned and stormed away. He could not bear to look at his wife today. And yet, through his rage, an inkling of understanding began to form. His wife was playing some game, not with him but with Ariadne Marshall. And Mrs. Marshall was almost certainly not playing fair.

WHEN FRANCES RETIRED for the night with the infant, Ariadne picked up the black veil she had abandoned on the chair and took it to her chamber. Here, Lawson helped her dress in the black silk and pinned on the veil with her diamond tiara. That is, it had once been set with diamonds before she had had to sell them and replace them with paste.

"You may retire," Ariadne told the maid as she left without explanation.

As soon as she entered the gaming club in the hotel's back room, she was glad of the veil, for among the many faces which turned to watch her were several that she recognized, including Lord Wickenden—the Wicked Baron himself—and young Lord Daxton who was probably even wickeder, and more likely to suit her purpose. But, she had learned her lesson from Torridon and had no intention of pursuing. She would let Daxton come to her if he was going to. Wickenden was probably too knowing to be useful. Besides, rumor said he had grown positively virtuous since his marriage.

The doorman had been right. This was not the sort of club ladies attended. The women here were largely courtesans, actresses, and dancers, she guessed, hanging on the arms of the wealthy and the winning. Ariadne strolled among them, contemplating if and where to play with the very little money left in her purse. Most of the games were for higher stakes than she could ever consider. Even Daxton, normally in a hurry to throw away his money or, occasionally, win it back, eschewed those tables. In fact, his ridiculously handsome face betrayed boredom more than anything else.

There was one nasty moment when a man pushed back his chair, only just missing her toes. Ariadne had no intention of making a fuss, since the man was Frances's brother, Lord Braithwaite. He apologized profusely for his clumsiness, but did not appear to recognize her through the thick veil. However, she had only recovered from that shock when Lord Torridon strode through the door.

Frowning blackly, he looked as if he were more inclined to start a fight than play games. Braithwaite called to him, and Ariadne hastily fished out her last sovereign and on impulse, leaned over the shoulder of a young gentleman playing E.O. and placed her coin on Odd.

"Just in time," the young gentleman murmured as the wheel spun.

Ariadne, quite prepared to lose, was delighted to find the ball finished on Odd.

"Drat, you won and I lost," the young man observed. "Now, should I follow your luck or my own?"

"I wouldn't follow mine," Ariadne said, amused. "I suspect I've just used it up for the next six months!" She scooped up her winnings with the help of the amiable young man who stood to present her with the rest. He gazed down at her veiled face with undisguised curiosity.

"What is your story, ma'am? What brings a widowed lady to such a den of vice?"

"Desperation," she said lightly, "and you see it has worked."

"I hate to think of any lady so desperate. Won't you let me be your guide and escort for the evening?"

"But I don't know who you are," she murmured, casting a quick glance toward the door. Lord Torridon was leaving again, with Braithwaite and Wickenden. They were probably all staying at the castle.

"Sylvester Gaunt," he replied with a quick, almost jerky bow. "And you are?"

"Mrs. Thom." She raised her eyes to his handsome, if reckless face once more and sighed. "I am companion to a very exacting lady. I dream of winning my way out of subservience."

"You won't do that here," Sylvester Gaunt said seriously. "Place is full of card sharps. And even where the table is honest, the odds are so stacked against you, you'll lose in the end."

"Then what are you doing here?" she asked tartly.

He grinned, very young and attractively boyish. "Having fun, of course."

My ideal companion…

FRANCES WOKE WITH her husband's name on her lips and her heart beating fast with excitement. Furious to be awake, for in her dream he had been about to make love to her, she lay staring at the ceiling, trying to gather herself before she responded to Jamie's cry.

She had not closed the bed curtains and daylight seeped through the windows. Rain pattered against the glass, reminding her that last year's spring ball had been in fine weather. She had been happy last year.

Rising, she went to the cot and gazed down at Jamie who stopped crying immediately and grinned at her.

"What a demanding, greedy little fellow you are," she said loving-ly, and reached down to pick him up.

Returning to bed to feed him, she listened to the rain and let her mind wander at will. She didn't quite understand why she wasn't happy any more. She had quarreled with Alan, of course, but that hadn't so much caused her unhappiness as resulted from it. She loved Alan. She always had. She loved Jamie and being his mother. She even liked Torridon and the people who lived there—with the possible exception of Lady Torridon who should really have taken herself back to her own establishment near Glasgow before now.

She liked being mistress of her own house… but she missed her siblings more than she had imagined. That Serena and Gervaise had both married since she had last seen them made her feel alone and disconnected. And the girls were growing up so quickly. And all these things happened while she'd been trapped at Torridon.

Only, no one else had trapped her. She had *allowed* herself to be trapped through her desire not to displease her husband. Which had hardly worked since all that happened was that she had exploded with resentment and quarreled with him, which was far worse.

From nowhere, it came to her that she did not *know* her husband. He had courted her with just enough latent passion to overwhelm her with love, had married her, and given her a child along with all his worldly goods. But he had never given himself.

Dreamily, she thought back to those heady, early days, of their wedding trip when he had first taught her the physical joys of love. He had been so gentle, so tender that she had never even thought of her mother's warnings of shock and pain and endurance. Instead, she had fallen deeper in love with him, craving more…

Looking back, she wondered now if his lovemaking had merely been polite. For he had never *lost* himself in loving her as she did in him. Even then, she had sensed a powerful passion that he had never fully indulged, never given free rein to. It had become an obsession with her to make him lose control, to show her his wilder nature. But it had never happened. Jamie had happened instead, and from the moment she had told him of her happy condition, he had never touched her again.

And she, left behind with the baby whenever he went anywhere, had begun to suspect he indulged himself elsewhere.

According to Mama, she should never know such things. If she could not avoid knowing, she should turn a blind eye. A husband's peccadilloes were beneath her.

Well, she could no longer live like this, pretending to be the submissive wife every gentleman wanted. She would tell him so. She would talk to him. She would seduce him and make him forget everyone else. She remembered so well the heat of his skin and the rippling muscle beneath. She ached to touch him again, to be held in his arms and feel his passion. To know the joy...

A knock at the door interrupted her daydreams, and Ariadne sailed into the room *en déshabillé*. "Ah, good, you are awake already. Do you remember that I had them lay aside some masks and dominos for you to look at in the draper's shop? They are much less expensive than the ones at the modiste across the road. Also, we need to hire a conveyance of some kind to take us up to the castle this evening. And it just struck me we do not have cards of invitation and I suppose some flunky will check when it is a masquerade."

"I have an invitation," Frances said. "My new sister-in-law sent me one most properly, although I declined with equal civility. They won't examine it, though, and no one is announced at a masquerade." She peered at her yawning friend. "You look tired. Did you go out last night?"

"I did. That is, I went to the disreputable party in the hotel and won a little money to contribute to our bill. Your brother was there, though he did not stay."

"Who else did you see?" It was silly, but she had a sudden burst of longing to see Torridon here, looking for her. Although he was bound to be angry about her taking Jamie all the way down to Devon without a by your leave, he would be much too proud to try to stop her. In fact, she doubted he cared enough, which was most lowering of all. In any case, he had no reason to leave Torridon, let alone come to Blackhaven.

"That I knew?" Ariadne said. "No one... oh, apart from a few. Dax was there. And Wickenden. And a young man called Sylvester Gaunt—do I know that name?"

"Gaunt? He's probably one of the Tamar brothers. Unsavory, by all accounts and to be avoided."

"Oh, fiddlesticks," Ariadne said. "I expect people say that about me all the time!"

Chapter Four

A S SOON AS the Dowager Countess of Torridon learned that John the coachman had returned, she sent for him.

John, who had quite enough courage and confidence to see off any danger encountered on the road, turned into a nervous schoolboy whenever he stood before the dowager. Twisting his hat in his hands, he waited for her to gaze her fill.

The countess, well aware of her effect, let him wait.

At last, she pronounced, "You did not bring young Lady Torridon back."

"No, my lady. She sent me back with the coach."

"What were you thinking of, taking her and my grandson any-where beyond the village?" the countess snapped.

"I just followed her instructions, my lady. It's what I'm paid for."

Lady Torridon glared. "You are not paid to drive my grandson away from his father and me! Where did you leave him?"

"With his mother, my lady, in perfect health," John assured her.

"Where?" she repeated.

"Edinburgh, my lady. Smart house in Charlotte Square. Belongs to a very good friend... A widow."

"Edinburgh?" she repeated. "But my son believes she has gone to her family in Blackhaven! Did you not see him on the road?"

"No, my lady."

Lady Torridon glared at him harder. "Honesty, if you please," she demanded. "Has she run away?"

"Oh no, my lady," came John's shocked response. "She gave me a letter for Himself."

The countess held out her hand.

John swallowed audibly. "It's addressed to his lordship."

"Who is in Blackhaven! Kindly give me the letter so that I can decide what is best to be done."

Reluctantly, John took the missive from his pocket and handed it to her.

Without compunction, she broke the seal and read.

My dear Torridon,

On impulse, I have come to Edinburgh with Jamie. I feel the change in scene will do us both good. As John will tell you, we are staying with Mrs. Marshall, who is a good friend to me, although I know you do not like her. There is no cause for your concern, since we shall both be back in a few days.

Ever yours,
Frances.

Just like the girl herself: informal, insolent, openly defiant. Lady Torridon still hadn't forgiven her for rejecting the wet nurse she had personally recommended. Feeding the child herself indeed, like some crofter's wench. And now... how dared she visit someone she knew her husband disliked? More than that, how dared she take his son there?

She frowned, raising her gaze to John's unquiet face. "If she is returning in a few days, why did she send you home?"

"I couldn't say, my lady," John muttered. "I believe she hired a post chaise."

"Then she's going on somewhere else? Where?"

"I did hear Blackhaven mentioned, my lady, but I really don't know," John said desperately.

"I don't like this," Lady Torridon fumed. "I don't like this at all." And yet... And yet, it brought things out into the open. "Wait a moment, this widow she is with, what is her name?"

"Mrs. Marshall, my lady."

"*Ariadne* Marshall? That woman!" With as much triumph as disgust, Lady Torridon spun away, beginning to see her way. "Have the carriage ready in an hour," she said. "I believe I need to see my man of business in Edinburgh."

WITH THE KNOWLEDGE that his wife and son were safe, Torridon slept better, and yet awoke with fresh pain and fury churning him up. He could not face breakfast and the strain of being polite to his hosts and fellow guests, so he donned his traveling clothes, determined to return immediately to Scotland.

Throwing himself into the chair by the desk, he picked up the pen and began to write a polite note of excuse.

My dear Lady Braithwaite, he began, then stared at the blank expanse of paper. With a groan, he threw down the pen, splattering ink over the page, which he then crumpled and threw across the room. If he wrote, he couldn't *not* mention the presence of his wife in Blackhaven.

Springing to his feet, he paced to the window and back several times.

"Damn you, damn you, damn you," he whispered over and over. He didn't even know if he was speaking to himself or his wife, or to Ariadne Marshall, whom he wanted to blame for the whole turn of events but couldn't.

He could storm down there in righteous fury and take his wife home by force. It would have to be home, for they could not play out their quarrel here in front of her family and their guests. But even supposing he could cow her into submission... did he really want a wife who stayed with him through fear? God help him, he didn't want to quarrel with Frances. He wanted her to run back to him, to be his.

He let out a laugh that sounded slightly demented to his own ears.

Something had gone wrong between them and he doubted he could fix it by playing the heavy-handed husband.

Abruptly, he seized his greatcoat and left the bedchamber. He ran down the main staircase and strode across the hall, determined to get out without speaking to anyone. Achieving that minor success, he strode on to the main drive. The rain didn't bother him. He lived, after all, in the west of Scotland.

Walking into Blackhaven, he came to the eventual conclusion that he couldn't leave yet. If Frances was in trouble via this game with Ariadne Marshall, he needed to help her before they tried to fix their marriage. Besides, it came to him that he could take a hand in the game, whatever it turned out to be. And so, he would buy a mask and attend tonight's ball, and find out what she was up to.

Arriving in the town soaking wet, he went into the coffee house in High Street to dry off a little. By chance, it was directly opposite the hotel, and he found himself gazing with disfavor at the first-floor windows. As a soldier, he had always kept his anger under control until it was needed for battle. That now seemed easy compared with dealing with his wife.

When the rain went off, he strolled across the road to the little draper's shop he'd passed on his way in. Walter Jones, Quality Draper, said the sign above the door.

Entering, Torridon found it even smaller than it looked. It took but two paces to the main counter, the rest of the space being taken up by cabinets and boxes.

The proprietor beamed upon him. "Good morning, sir. How might I help you?"

Torridon cast a doubtful glance at the display case, containing largely handkerchiefs and ribbons. "I don't suppose you have such silly things as masks and domino cloaks suitable for a masquerade ball?"

"Of course, sir, of course. And at a much better price, I must say, than you will find elsewhere in the town. Nor do we skimp on quality. Perhaps sir has a particular color in mind?"

"Lord no, I don't care."

The draper, presumably Mr. Walter Jones himself, climbed a ladder and took down a box.

"Your shop is new, is it not?" Torridon asked. "I don't recall seeing it before."

"It is, sir. I moved here from Whalen some eight or nine months ago now, and I have to say business is better. Are you a frequent visitor, then, sir?"

"No, though perhaps I should be." He glanced at the box of masks opened by Mr. Jones and grabbed the first one.

"Try it on, sir," Mr. Jones said, scandalized. "You don't want something too small for your face."

Torridon, who didn't actually care one way or the other, had the time to indulge him. He tied on the mask and glanced in the mirror set on the counter. He looked more like a highwayman than a gentleman going to a ball.

Just then, the shop door opened again and a widow came in. She, too, paused in apparent surprise at the size of the establishment, then approached the counter. Something in her movement triggered an elusive memory.

Torridon bowed to her as best he could in the cramped space, and the lady's breath caught. It struck him that she was trying not to laugh, though she inclined her head in civil response.

"I shall be with you in one moment, madam," Mr. Jones assured her. But Torridon, intrigued, pressed himself back against the cabinets, gesturing with one hand that she should be served first.

The widow, a young woman by the way she moved, inclined her head to him again with perfect gravity, although it struck him she was still amused.

"I'm Mrs. Alan," she said to the draper with the faintest quiver in her voice, and Torridon's mouth fell open. He hadn't recognized his own wife. "I believe my friend Mrs. Thom asked you to put aside a few masks and domino cloaks?"

"Ah yes, of course, madam," Jones said. "One moment."

While Torridon stared at his wife in her widow's weeds, Jones ducked under the counter so quickly that he might have collapsed. Frances, presumably fearing the same thing, stood on tiptoe to peer over the top. Mr. Jones popped back up again and she jerked back, narrowly missing a clash of heads.

An involuntary hiss of laughter escaped Torridon. Beneath her veil, his wife seemed to cast him another glance. He could almost swear her eyes laughed back, although he could barely see them through the thickness of the veil. Did she recognize him, too?

He held his breath while Jones placed several cloaks and masks on the counter.

"Mrs. Thom," the draper said, "preferred the gold cloak and mask."

Good for Ariadne, Torridon thought irritably. Presumably she expected Frances to pay for her preferences.

"Yes, so she told me," Frances said. "We shall definitely take those. Oh, and this dark blue domino will be perfect with my gown. Is there a mask to match?"

"Sadly, not exactly, but either of these blues would blend wonderfully. Or you could try a contrast with this silver one perhaps?"

Under Torridon's fascinated gaze, Frances considered them all against the cloak. Abruptly, she glanced up at him, perhaps irritated by his scrutiny.

"Try them on." The words spilled from his lips unbidden. More, he spoke them in an unnaturally husky voice, and with the oft-mimicked accent of a mad Cossack officer he had once met in his army days.

Mr. Jones blinked at him in surprise. However, perhaps because it would have been his own advice anyway, he beamed. "An excellent idea." Lifting the mirror from its place in front of Torridon, he set it before Frances instead.

She swung the blue domino about her shoulders, and lifted her veil.

She took Torridon's breath away. She always had. There was nothing ordinary about Frances's beauty. It came from within, shining with fun and mischief and innate kindness. And passion, that, too. She was everything he had ever wanted, ever needed. And more, so much more…

Under his avid gaze, she held each of the blue masks against her face in turn.

"Allow me," Torridon offered and caught the strings of the current mask, drawing them behind her head. He needed, suddenly, to touch her.

No, she did not know him. He felt her stiffen very slightly at the light brush of his fingers against her veil. Not her hair.

He paused. "You are in deep mourning, madam," he observed.

She blinked, as though she had forgotten the normal purpose of her widow's weeds. "Oh well, it is dull to mourn all the time," she blurted. The words might have been spoken by Ariadne Marshall.

"Then, if you do not intend to wear the veil with the mask," Torridon said, "might I suggest you remove it for now?"

She raised her hands to unpin it, but again he was ahead of her, deftly removing the correct pins as he so often had. To him, it was a gesture of intimacy, of possession, and he suspected she wasn't entirely comfortable. She had no idea who he was. It hurt him and thrilled him at the same time. He could be anyone he wished to be with her. Like this, he carried no baggage of marital quarrels or recrimination. He could tease her, court her. Play her game… or his own.

However, unwilling to frighten her, he took no impudent advantage of his position. In fact, to set her at ease, he even included the draper himself in the discussion. "What do you think, Mr. Jones? Is that blue not just a little insipid with such brilliant eyes?"

"Perhaps it does not suit madam's coloring as well as it should," the draper said tactfully. "Why don't you try the darker blue?"

Again, Torridon could touch the soft, silky hair at the back of her head. She had relaxed more, seeming undisturbed by his nearness, though not, he could swear, unaware. Secretly, he inhaled her scent of orange blossom and vanilla, drowned in memory and longing, while he behaved like a perfect gentleman.

In the end, they all agreed on the contrasting silver mask, and Mr. Jones again dropped like a stone behind the counter in order, presumably, to wrap her purchases. Torridon leaned over the counter to be sure. The ingenious draper had a little table down there, which rolled out on wheels from under the counter. On it were balls of string and scissors. Grinning, Torridon glanced back at Frances. Her eyes sparked with responsive laughter, though she pulled her lips into an expression of strict gravity.

"I take it you will be a guest at the Braithwaite spring ball?" she said breathlessly.

"Oh, no," he replied at once.

She blinked and gestured delicately toward his mask.

"This?" he said, touching it as though he had forgotten its existence. "A tool of my trade, madam. I am a highwayman."

She cast him a doubtful glance, as though she half-believed him. Certainly, his wet old clothing was not that of a man of fashion, and not how he normally appeared before her. But neither was she foolish. Her eyes teased him. "Are you planning to rob Mr. Jones or me?" she inquired.

"Neither," he replied in shocked tones. "I would not dream of stepping on the toes of urban thieves."

"Of course, you would not. Forgive my unwitting insult. I expect your old mask broke."

"I expect it did," he agreed.

"While you held up someone terribly wealthy," she added, warming to her story as she often did, indulging in wildly unlikely and often highly amusing flights of fancy.

"Disgustingly wealthy," he agreed.

"So, did you run away before he could see your face?" she asked innocently.

"Oh no," Torridon said, as though shocked by such misunderstanding. "I robbed him blind. I couldn't be expected to forego such fantastical wealth."

She nodded. "Of course not. I quite see that. But aren't you afraid he will recognize you?"

"Not a bit," Torridon said blithely. "I shot him."

Frances let out a choke of surprised laughter, and Torridon smiled back. He had missed his wife. He ached to make her fall in love with him all over again.

"Get along with you, sir," Mr. Jones exclaimed, his voice muffled and vaguely sepulchral down behind the counter. "You must not be frightening my female customers."

One parcel slithered across the counter in front of Frances, pushed from below. She looked hastily away from Torridon before laughter could consume her.

"I don't believe the lady is afraid of me," he assured Jones, who popped back up at that moment with the second parcel.

"Thank you," Frances said unsteadily. "I'll take them with me now."

While she paid, Torridon regretted not being able to carry her parcels to the hotel for her. It would involve removing his mask. So, he merely held the door open for her as she left.

"Goodbye," she said brightly. "I expect I *shall* see you at the castle tonight."

"If I choose to rob it after all."

"Of course. I hope you will spare me." She sailed out without a backward glance. But he was sure she was smiling. As he was. Because now he had a reason to attend the ball. Not just to find out what she was up to, but to court her.

Chapter Five

I T SEEMED BOTH strange and exciting to drive up to her own home as a stranger, to walk up the front steps, and be directed to the ballroom, once the medieval castle's great hall. As she and Ariadne waited patiently behind a large blue domino and an even larger pink one, Frances wanted to laugh, because there in the mezzanine gallery, running around behind the orchestra, were her three little sisters, behaving almost exactly as she had once done with Gervaise and Serena, desperate to catch a glimpse of the fashionable guests and those long ago, magical spring balls from which they were supposed to be excluded.

Straightening her face so that she didn't give her sisters' game away to her mother or sister-in-law, she prepared to be welcomed.

The new Countess of Braithwaite was undeniably beautiful, with red-blonde hair like a Highland sunrise, and a gaze at once shy and direct. Her brilliant green eyes were particularly lovely behind the jeweled mask, but they also held humor, and her lips were used to smiling. Frances thought she would like her.

In response to the countess's greeting, Frances opted for a small, mysterious smile and a silent curtsey. She wasn't entirely sure such tactics would work on Gervaise or her mother who stood at his other side.

Neither Gervaise nor the dowager countess were wearing masks. Frances looked each boldly in the eye as she curtsied and smiled, prepared to burst into delighted laughter as soon as they recognized her. She was almost disappointed when neither did. Gervaise seemed more concerned with how his wife coped with what was no doubt her first major social duty, and the dowager countess had far too much dignity to pry into the identity behind the masks. No doubt she disapproved of the whole thing. Serena, and possibly Eleanor, the new countess, had obviously talked her into it. Or overruled her.

"Drat it, you are too good at this," Ariadne murmured in her ear. "Your own mother does not know you!"

"Shall we call it another draw?" Frances suggested.

"Certainly not. The night is young." Ariadne glided away, much to France's amused frustration. If they did not stay together, how would they know if the other was recognized? Trust, she supposed, accepting a glass of champagne from Harry, the second footman, with a murmur of thanks. He didn't recognize her either. As she had told Ariadne, it was all a matter of expectation, and no one expected her to be here.

It was much easier from her own point of view. She picked out Serena quite easily, play-flirting with her fan for the delectation of an older gentleman who was surely Mr. Winslow. And there, by the open terrace door, with the midnight black hair, was Kate Crowmore who had inexplicably married the new vicar of Blackhaven's church. Her old friend Gillie was dancing with none other than Dax, the same Lord Daxton who had once almost ruined Serena. How come he was even invited?

Up on the gallery, as the music ended, the girls waved to someone below. Frances suspected it was Miss Grey, their old governess who had married the tenant of Haven Hall. Subtly, the lady made a shooing gesture with her fan while turning to speak politely to her masked partner. It seemed the children rightly trusted her not to give them away.

Frances couldn't help smiling. She wondered if she could sneak up there and swear the children to secrecy. Tonight, even Maria seemed very much the mischievous child, so much so that Frances wondered if she was mistaken in her suspicions about the young officer.

"Now, I am devastated," claimed a foreign yet definitely familiar voice next to her.

With an unexpected thrill of pleasure, Frances turned and beheld a tall man in a scarlet cloak and a black mask. It could indeed have been the same masked face she had seen in the draper's shop. It certainly sounded like him. Although by what she glimpsed of his clothes beneath the domino, he was now much better dressed.

He placed his hand over his heart in a gesture both humorous and rueful. "I thought you were smiling at me. And now I see such favor is bestowed instead upon the orchestra."

Frances laughed, for he was almost right. "Do I have reason to smile at you?" she asked. "Do you know me, sir?"

His lips curved in a slow, beguiling smile. His eyes, half-shadowed behind the mask, leapt with innate turbulence. For no reason that she could fathom, her heart thudded.

"No," he said. "Not yet. Beyond the fact that I did not rob you."

So, it *was* the man from the draper's shop.

"I cannot see the point of waiting for someone else to introduce us," he said. "Especially since you smiled at me."

"Only I didn't."

"You did in the shop. And you might again, if you got to know me."

"I might dislike you intensely," she countered.

"Shall we dance, and see which way the wind blows?"

She could already feel her lips trying to curve, so she accepted gracefully. After all, it was a ball. Dancing was the main purpose. Her partner took the champagne glass from her fingers and set it down on the nearest table. The orchestra, as though commanded by him, struck up a waltz.

As his arm encircled her waist, excitement soared. It seemed a lifetime ago that she had last waltzed, and yet she loved dancing. Her partner held her like a perfect gentleman should although he danced with a touch more flamboyance than she was used to.

"You are not English, are you?" she observed.

His lips quirked. "No, I am not."

"Where are you from?"

"Guess," he challenged.

"I think your accent is Russian."

He inclined his dark head. "Your ear is good... or my English is bad. Yes, the accent is Russian. And where are *you* from, madam?"

"I was born nearby."

"Ah, you are a local lady."

She raised her eyebrows. "Is that bad?"

"Not in the least. I shall be able to call on you during my stay."

"But you don't know where I shall be."

He smiled and spun her around. "I shall discover your name at the unmasking,"

She smiled back. "Perhaps."

They danced in silence for a few moments. His hand was warm at her back. Behind the mask, his eyes glittered. She guessed they, like he, was permanently stormy in character. Which was strangely exciting, like his foreignness, his sheer differentness.

"So where is your husband, madam?" he asked softly.

"He is not here."

The mask moved, as if his eyebrows had flown up. "He did not wish the honor of escorting you?"

"He has more important things to do than dance at silly masquerades," she said lightly.

"Then he is a dull dog." It wasn't quite a question.

Irritated, Frances snapped, "Of course he is not. And at this moment, I do not see *you* dancing attendance on *your* wife."

He smiled. "You might yet be surprised. But how do you know I have one? And if I had, how could I attend her and you at the same time?"

"I don't know, but I would like to see you try."

"Do I perceive a cruel streak in you, madam? Or merely a healthy sense of the ridiculous?"

"Guess," she invited, echoing his earlier challenge, and he let out a hiss of laughter.

"Now I have to know you better. Will you dance with me again?

The supper dance, perhaps."

"I don't know," she said honestly. The hired carriage was ordered to return at midnight, but she could have already fled by then, or be discovered and in disgrace. Or handing over the Torridon rubies to let Ariadne strut off to some gaming hell in them.

"You are awaiting a better offer?" he guessed, his voice curiously flat.

"Oh no, that would be rude. To be truthful, sir, you intrigue me, so I would like to dance with you again, but my life is complicated. There are circumstances beyond my control."

His eyes narrowed, then lifted, as though gazing about them for some threat. "What circumstances?"

Touched by the stranger's concern, she said, "Oh, I assure you, I am not in *danger*. Except of doing something foolish."

"Such as what?"

"Repeating mistakes," she said ruefully.

His eyes held hers. For a moment, she felt dizzy, as though she knew him, as though he saw everything about her in that one penetrating, stormy glance.

"What heinous mistake can you possibly have committed?" he asked, sounding more foreign than ever. She did not think he was French or Spanish or Italian. And he did not sound German. Perhaps he was Swedish. Or Russian. With difficulty, she dragged her mind back to his question.

"I act on impulse," she confessed, "and then cannot go back on my word."

"Have you promised something you cannot give?"

"I have promised something I *should* not give," she said ruefully. "Or even lend, which is what I wagered."

"Lending is not irreversible," he pointed out.

"True, but that is not the height of my crime."

"So much sin in one small lady," he teased. "Tell me all and I shall make it go away."

For a moment, she was actually tempted. His eyes had calmed, leaving them almost familiar, and his voice was so kind... But the light moved as they danced, casting half his face into shadow for an instant. And she remembered that he was a stranger, and that she didn't even know what she wanted or how to achieve it. More than that, there was a hint of danger in his flirting, a purpose she could only guess at, and though it excited her, she was also wary.

"You are very good," she said at last. "But I believe I want to fix it by myself."

He inclined his head. "If you need help, you can find me here."

"In the ballroom?" she teased.

"Wherever you wish. For instance, we could meet on the terrace in a little over one hour—just before the supper dance."

She stared at him, curiously disappointed. "That sounds more like an assignation than an offer to help."

"Does it matter what you call it, so long as it is what you want?" His thumb moved, softly caressing her gloved hand.

She tilted her chin. "But it isn't what I want in the slightest. I believe I am fatigued and would prefer to sit out the rest of the dance."

For no reason that she could fathom, he smiled. Was he actually glad to be rejected? Despite the heat in his eyes and his voice?

"Forgive my forwardness. I shall not ask again, if you choose to finish our dance. Though I confess I want nothing more than to be alone with you while I hold you in my arms, closer than this."

"That will never happen," she said flatly. "I am a married woman, sir. Vulgar liaisons hold no charm for me."

His expression was secretive again, yet the turbulence still raged behind his eyes. He said, "Your husband is a lucky man."

Her lips twisted. "I wish he was."

He was silent for a few moments, then, "I will help you, you know, with or without assignations."

"You are kind," she said with a quick smile. "I think. Are you a soldier, sir?"

He blinked, no doubt at the sudden change of subject. "How did you guess?"

"There is something familiar in the way you hold yourself." *And me.*

LORD TORRIDON HAD recognized his wife as soon as she entered the ballroom. It wasn't difficult since she wore the same dark blue domino and silver mask she had bought from Mr. Jones this morning.

When Frances arrived, he was lounging against the wall near the entrance, single-mindedly watching the new arrivals. It was something of a miracle that she didn't spot him at once, too. He was sure Ariadne Marshall did. But Frances was acting now, her attention all focused on making sure none of her family recognized her through the mask. At least she and Mrs. Marshall did not cling to each other, but went their separate ways. And Torridon followed his wife.

Of course, he was discreet. Whatever she was up to, whatever trouble she was in, or was causing, he had no desire to create a scandal. And so, he strolled after her, watching only out of the corner of his eye, to see if she was looking for anyone, meeting anyone…

In several bouts of painful jealousy, he had already tortured himself with the possibility that she had come home to Blackhaven in disguise in order to meet some old lover in secret, someone to whom she would rather be married. Though he struggled to think who this could be. Most of the dashing officers once barracked in the town had been sent to join Wellington on the Peninsula last year and had not yet returned home.

Of course, it did not have to be a local man. It could be some fashionable London guest staying at the castle or in the town. But her gaze glossed over Lord Wickenden, who was the likeliest candidate to Torridon's mind, and rested briefly on Lord Daxton. However, there was nothing loverlike in her observation—the opposite, in fact.

She seemed more interested in the children cavorting in the gallery. It was the way she smiled to herself that made his heart turn over, and although he hadn't meant to approach her this early in the evening, he did, dredging the words from somewhere, and the accent, as before, from the mad Russian captain with whom he had enjoyed a crazy night of adventure.

He didn't know whether to be delighted or appalled when Frances responded as she did. But even the most exacting husband could hardly condemn his wife for accepting an invitation to dance at a ball. Their conversation thrilled and unnerved him, flooding him with emotion, because for the first time in months he held her in his arms. It was a most strange encounter, because although they were both pretending, and she clearly had no idea who he was, he had the impression that on some level, they were both being honest. As one could only be with strangers.

She did not appear to mind his boldness or the freedom of the way he chose to dance. In fact, he was sure she was about to tell him why she was here before she clammed up. In retrospect, trying to make an assignation with her might have been a mistake. At the time, he hadn't even known whether or not he wanted her to accept. Having deliberately enticed her, though, he could hardly admit to his true identity.

Why didn't she guess? *He* had known *her* immediately, even behind the concealing veil. Was a mask, a fake Russian accent, and a deliberate huskiness in his voice truly enough to fool a loving wife?

"Are you a soldier, sir?" she asked curiously, at last.

"How did you guess?"

"Something familiar in the way you hold yourself."

A breath of laughter took him by surprise. He realized suddenly that he carried himself differently as a civilian. By adopting Captain Savarin's accent, he seemed to have re-found something of his old life, from the days when he had known what he was doing and could look after a company of men in battle far more easily than he could take care of his own wife or the estate that should have been Andrew's. Andrew's death had brought him home to grieve, and to take up the reluctant reigns of his responsibility as earl. He, Alan, was the one who had chosen to risk his life in war. It should not have been Andrew who died.

Frances, so full of fun and happiness, had lifted him out of that trough and given him hope. He'd never told her that, merely tried his best to be a worthy husband to her. And somehow, he had failed. She had not retained her happiness with him. In that instant, despite the anger and frustration still simmering away within him, he would have willingly died just to bring back her joy. His arms ached to fold her against him. For the first time, he hated the dishonesty of this meeting. He wanted it to be in private, face to face with no masks, only truth between them.

But he could only gaze down at his wife's beautiful face, at once dearly familiar and utterly mysterious.

"I wonder," he said, "if we are blinded by faces, and only see the person beneath when that face is hidden?"

Her lips quirked upward in the start of the smile he loved. "That is a very profound observation for a masked ball."

"I am profundity incarnate," he said flippantly.

Her smile broadened and died. Something, a frown perhaps, tugged at her embroidered silver mask. "Someone has hurt you by dishonesty."

He almost stumbled. "That would be harsh," he managed at last, only just hanging on to his accent. "I cannot tell what is her dishonesty and what is my own blindness."

She stared at him. For an instant, he thought she had seen through the mask at last, and tried to prepare for whatever deluge of fury or grief or fear was about to engulf them. He would have to take her quickly out of the crowd—onto the terrace perhaps, despite its unenticing cold and dampness.

But her eyes, glistening with unshed tears, were not seeing him. And their dance was coming to an end.

She tried to smile. "I think you have helped me after all, sir."

As the music finished, their hands parted and he released her. He bowed from habit, though every nerve was thrown into panic because she was about to walk away from him.

She said, "I hope you might solve your troubles, too. And I hope we meet again."

"As do I," he managed.

And then she was gone, flitting through the ballroom like a butterfly through a field of flowers. He had no idea where she was going, but he didn't want her to leave.

"SHE'S HERE," HE told Lord Braithwaite a few minutes later when they encountered each other near the cardroom door.

"Here? At the ball?" Braithwaite's shoulders sagged with relief for a moment before he straightened them again. "Thank God. How did she get past me? Not to mention my mother!"

"By acting. Neither of you were expecting her. You were greeting shiploads of people at the same time."

"Then how did *you* spot her?"

"I danced with her," Torridon said vaguely. Since Braithwaite had seemed convinced his sister would turn up in Blackhaven safe and well within the next day or so, and had not seemed inclined to worry, Torridon hadn't mentioned discovering her at the hotel last night, or the draper's this morning. Besides, some silly yet unshakeable belief that he was keeping faith with his wife by keeping her secret held him silent. "If it's any consolation to you, *she* didn't know *me*."

"What the devil is she up to?" Braithwaite demanded.

"I'm not sure," Torridon said, "but I suspect it involves Ariadne Marshall, who is also here."

"Where?" Braithwaite frowned as he scoured the ballroom.

In spite of everything, laughter caught in Torridon's throat. "Don't scowl at your guests. Braithwaite, you'll scare them off. Mrs. Marshall is the lady in the gold domino, flirting with Tamar's brother."

Braithwaite's lip curled slightly. "Lord. Not sure who I would back in that fight."

"She'd eat him alive."

"He's young," Braithwaite allowed. "But even he admits he's old in sin. Tamar's siblings are not terribly like him for the most part. One of his brothers, according to Serena, is a thief, and one of his sisters has almost certainly run off with a French spy. Although that is between you and me," he added with a hasty if slightly belated glance over his shoulder for eavesdroppers.

"Well, I suspect they can each look after themselves and we need not worry."

Braithwaite lowered his voice. "Do we need to worry about Frances? Is she in trouble of some kind?"

"I think she is," Torridon said slowly, "but I don't think it endangers her." With an effort, he smiled and clapped his brother-in-law on the back. "Go and dance with your wife, and let me look out for mine. I give you my word, I will."

Braithwaite nodded and began to move on, before he gestured across the ballroom to a group of young gentlemen blatantly ogling the ladies. Even over this distance, and with the orchestra playing, they were clearly too loud, having probably imbibed rather too much of Braithwaite's punch. One of them wore the uniform of the local regiment beneath his domino.

"I know I didn't recognize my own sister," Braithwaite said, "but I don't believe I know those fellows either. Neither does Tamar. If you see them step out of line, send to Paton, would you? He'll have them—er—escorted from the premises."

Torridon nodded. He had caught sight of his wife again, talking animatedly to Lord Tamar, whom she had not previously met. Torridon could not prevent his silly surge of jealousy, even though he understood what she was doing—examining the new members of her family. Having scrutinized her sister's husband, she moved on to her brother's wife, with whom she managed to strike up a conversation by the champagne table.

The latter conversation was interrupted by two of the four men Braithwaite had pointed out as uninvited guests. They were clearly trying to inveigle the ladies into the supper dance. Instinctively,

Torridon moved closer, ready to send the men about their business. But the ladies themselves managed that. With perfectly courteous smiles, they appeared to be claiming prior engagements and walked away arm in arm.

One of the men scowled and stumbled slightly as he turned. His friend grabbed his elbow and hauled him off onto the terrace for some much-needed fresh air. Hopefully, they would then find their way out of the castle before supper and the subsequent unmasking.

Torridon went in search of his wife, wondering if he could take her into the supper dance after all. He was fairly sure Ariadne Marshall would not miss the chance of a free meal, although the pair would no doubt flee after that to avoid the unmasking. Unless Torridon spoke to his wife and ended the charade now...

By the time the dance began, he had not found her, although Mrs. Marshall was dancing with Sylvester Gaunt. Torridon glanced up at the gallery, wondering if she had gone up there to greet her little sisters in secret, but there was no sign now of the children. Perhaps they had got bored, or been hauled off to bed by their governess. Or by Frances.

He turned, and something by the French window caught his eye— a flash of midnight blue as someone slipped outside. Frances.

It felt like as if someone had knocked him down and started to carve out his heart. She hadn't refused his assignation through loyalty, let alone love for her husband. She had refused it because she was meeting someone else. He had misread everything. Again. Everything he had imagined of her secret troubles, her innate honesty— honesty!—was false.

Before he knew it, he was striding after her, murderous rage in his heart.

Chapter Six

LADY MARIA CONWAY longed to be one of the masked dancers below. She wanted to waltz in the arms of Lieutenant Gideon Heath, although she couldn't help feeling it would be even more romantic to be courted by a mysterious stranger whose identity she could not guess. On the other hand, the lieutenant looked very dashing in his black mask and domino... though, somewhat ill-naturedly, she didn't like to see him enjoying himself quite so much. Perhaps he was merely as excited as she about their assignation, and he could hardly lean against the wall and scowl at everyone like Frances's husband. Where was Frances, when Torridon was here?

Actually, now that she thought about it, she would rather like Gideon to adopt a pose similar to Torridon's, and simply stare longingly up at her...

"Such a stupid rule," she said discontentedly to her younger sisters as they skulked behind the orchestra. "Just because I am not 'out,' I cannot attend our own ball."

"Frances and Serena didn't until they were seventeen," Alice pointed out. "And Gervaise was nineteen."

"Age does not matter," Maria said, but absently, for below, at last, Lieutenant Heath looked up and caught her eye and her breath. Subtly, he leaned his head toward the ballroom door, and her heart soared. She turned to her sisters. "Keep watch here while I check the way is clear. Once I come back, we can sneak outside and see how close we can come to the terrace."

"I think I should go with you," Alice pronounced, just as though she suspected something.

"Oh no, you must look after Helen, for you know we are not meant to be here either. I won't be long."

She slipped out of the gallery and ran along the passage and up-stairs to her new bedchamber. She no longer had to sleep in the nursery with Alice and Helen, which gave her a great deal more privacy.

From the back of her drawer she pulled out Gideon's gift—a pink embroidered mask and matching domino. Hastily, she tied on the mask and swung the cloak around her. She already knew the disguise was not enough for the ball itself. She could not pin up her own hair with enough expertise, and she could not even lift her arm without revealing that beneath the cloak she wore only a dull, everyday gown suitable only for a schoolroom miss. But when she drew up the hood, it was certainly good enough to hide her from the few servants and guests she might encounter straying from the ballroom.

She hurried out of her chamber once more and flitted back down-stairs to the row of reception rooms that ran between the ballroom and the entrance hall. As she had suspected, they were quiet at this time, since all the guests had arrived by now and it was nowhere near time for them to leave.

She lurked in the blue salon, her heart beating hard until the famil-iar red-coated figure strolled into view. His black cloak hung rakishly off one shoulder, revealing his fine regimental uniform, and he still wore his black mask.

"Gideon," she hissed.

He grinned and swerved out of the light into the dim part of the room where she waited. She threw herself into his arms, which closed about her at once. She smelled the wine on his breath as he kissed her, which wasn't as pleasant as she had hoped, but she was still too euphoric to object.

"I can't believe we've managed to meet here," she crowed. "Right under the noses of my mother and brother and sisters!"

He grinned. "You are a naughty little puss."

It wasn't quite how she wanted him to think of her, but she let it go. He didn't seem to be quite himself, for his eyes held a strange glitter, almost like a fever, and he spoke a little oddly, too. But he waltzed her around the room, quite out of time with the country dance being played in the ballroom, and made her laugh, especially when he bumped into the arm chair by the fireplace.

"I can't stay long," she said regretfully, "Alice and Helen will come looking for me if I don't go back directly. But we're going to sneak outside, soon, so I might see you on the terrace... if I can swear them to secrecy."

"I'll be there," Gideon said, letting her go to extract a flask from inside his coat. He took a sizeable swig.

"Gideon, are you foxed?" she asked with more interest than condemnation.

He grinned again. "Devil a bit. I'd offer you a sip, but I seem to have finished it. Give me another kiss."

"I can't," she murmured, backing off as her keen ears picked up distant childish voices. "My sisters are coming. Go back, go back."

"Maria," he expostulated, following. But she fled in the direction of the voices. Behind her, he laughed, and she was actually relieved that his footsteps moved away from her, back toward the ballroom.

She wasn't sure she cared for him foxed. Or perhaps she was just feeling guilty about lying to her sisters. Maybe she should take them into her confidence...

FRANCES HAD NOTICED almost as soon as the children had vanished from the gallery. She doubted that either their mother or their governess—if they even had a governess these days—had dragged them off. Which meant they were probably up to mischief. They did appear to be following a similar path as she and Serena had years earlier. And so, Frances peeped frequently out through the French window to see if they had strayed into the gardens or onto the terrace.

She and Serena had done so once during a spring ball when she was about ten years old. They had giggled all week because they had seen two people kissing who were not even married, or at least not to each other.

"Well?" Ariadne inquired, falling into step beside Frances as she made her way toward the window once more. "Anything to report?"

"I passed a glass of champagne to my mother, and admired Serena's gown. Both of them smiled at me without seeing me. Neither the Wickendens nor Dax, nor any of our neighbors, appear to have recognized me either. What about you?"

"Nothing definite, though I caught your brother looking at me once. He might be trying to work out how he knows me. You might yet win."

"I suspect it will be another stalemate. I don't know whether we should feel piqued or pat ourselves on the back for cleverness."

Ariadne laughed. "Oh, the latter, definitely the latter."

As Ari glided away again, Frances glanced out of the French window. And yes, there they were, three figures in the torchlight, flitting up the steps from the formal garden to the terrace. She would have let them catch whichever couple was brave enough to face the damp for love, except that the far end of the terrace was quite blatantly occupied by four young men who seemed to have given up on glasses and were drinking straight from wine bottles. Gervaise's wine bottles.

Go back, she willed her sisters. *Run back around the house and inside...*

But although they must have heard the drunken laughter, they did not perceive the danger. They stood there at top of the steps from the garden, the two younger ones behind Maria, who was laughing breathlessly. Lit by the torchlight from the covered terrace, with only a few raindrops glistening on their hair, they were so beautiful and appealing that Frances's heart swelled.

Maria, saw the men first. Her smile faltered. She looked poised to run. But she didn't.

Frances whisked herself outside, just as one of the men said, "By

George, what have we here? What's your name, my pretty?"

"There's three of them," another pointed out, slurring. "Almost one for each of us." They lurched toward the girls, but Frances was closer, quicker, and steadier on her feet. Tears had started to Maria's eyes, and Frances wanted to hug her, for she suddenly understood. One of the drunks was surely the same officer who had asked her to dance a little too forcefully earlier in the evening. With dismay, she realized he must be the soldier she had seen Frances with that first day. If Maria fancied herself in love with the idiot, the disappointment must have been immense.

For now, all Frances could do was protect them all. Standing in front of her sisters, she murmured. "Run back the way you came or the countess will see you. Now."

As she had expected, the threat of their mother's ire trumped both curiosity and bravery. In truth, the younger ones probably imagined the men's only threat was telling their mother they were here. But Maria would have seen already that her admirer had feet of clay— which was probably a good thing.

The girls fled back into the darkness. Helen's whispered, "Don't tell!" came back to her on the breeze.

The four men now standing between her and the ballroom, looked baffled. The officer was frowning, gazing owlishly in the direction where Maria had once stood.

"For a moment, there were four of them," one man said, scratching his head. "Which was just right." He peered owlishly beyond Frances.

"*She* frightened the other fillies away," slurred another, taking a swig from his bottle.

"Those *fillies* are children," Frances said with contempt. "Moreover, they are the sisters of your host. I suggest you sober up and go home before Lord Braithwaite discovers your disrespect."

The first man giggled. "*She* scared them off to have the pick of us herself."

"Can't assume that, old man," the officer said with a shade of unease. "Though I have to say she's a damned fine woman."

"I hear perfectly, too," Frances said wryly. "Excuse me, gentlemen, you are blocking my way."

She stepped forward in the belief that they would instinctively move aside. But whether their reactions were too slow, or the drink had already made them too insolent, they all stayed where they were and she now found herself far too close to four young bucks, convinced by alcohol that they were irresistible to the opposite sex. Combined with the freedom accorded by their masks, and the pack animal instincts already to the fore, insult of some kind seemed inevitable.

But she was the Countess of Torridon, the daughter of generations of earls, and she refused to be intimidated.

"I believe I asked you to stand aside," she said coldly.

She tried to step around them, only the man with the bottle moved to block her. She had a sudden horror that they would encircle her like wolves and tear her apart one way or another. Well, they would not get off easily, for Gervaise had once told her, after an alarming incident with an ungentlemanly rake in London, how best to disable a man.

"Cretin," she uttered when he lifted his hand, and poised her knee to damage him.

Abruptly, the man's reaching arm was knocked up. A large hand landed on his chest and shoved hard. He staggered backward into his fellows looking more astonished than alarmed.

"They are all miserable cretins," snapped her savior, a man with a strange accent wearing a scarlet domino and a black mask. The Russian stood beside her, lending her fresh courage, along with an unlikely sense of safety. "Perhaps you would care to go inside, madam, while I teach them some manners."

"I shall be pleased to accompany *you* inside, sir," she said at once. Her aim was to prevent physical violence, but it seemed her rescuer had other ideas.

"Then step back," he said with a hint of grimness, "for my lessons tend to be large."

For some reason she wanted to laugh—hysteria, no doubt—but as she obeyed, the drunken officer took exception to her rescuer.

"Manners?" he repeated, affronted. "I have no need to be taught manners by some Johnny Foreigner! I demand an apology, sir, or satisfaction!"

The Johnny Foreigner punched him in the jaw, hard enough to send him staggering into his nearest friend. They both fell, sprawling on the damp terrace.

"Thank you, that was most satisfying," Frances's rescuer said with rather frightening pleasure as he turned on the other two, kicking the nearest in the rear. Frances found it quite satisfying, too, since she suspected the struck officer of meeting Maria clandestinely.

"Be gone!" the Russian roared. "Braithwaite's men are already looking for you."

With that, he spun around as though he'd done no more than set a chair for someone, and offered Frances his arm. Her fingers shook slightly as she placed them on his sleeve and walked around the struggling, sprawling bodies toward the French door. He had obvious-ly closed it on his way out, perhaps to prevent the noise of a fight reaching the ballroom.

"Thank you," she whispered. "You must think me very foolish to have gone out there."

His arm was stiff under her fingers, his body tense. She thought he was angry with her as much as with the drunks he had dealt with so summarily. But he didn't reply, for as he opened the French door, Serena all but bumped into them, looking frantic.

"Is anyone else out there?" Serena demanded. "I'm sure I heard shouting. I've lost my young sisters and they're not in their beds!"

"I suspect they will be by now," Frances said, remembering to speak in the soft, Scottish voice she had been using to people she knew. "I sent them inside…"

Her rescuer's gaze seemed to burn into her face. Perhaps he had suspected her of another assignation and was now mortified—as he should have been.

As Serena hurried off, Frances said, "I am a silly woman, but not quite stupid."

"It is I who am stupid," he said ruefully, leading her into an alcove. "*You* are kind and brave." His lips quirked beneath the mask. "Though I had not realized you were Scottish."

She sank onto one of the chairs. "Only by marriage. I'm hiding from the Braithwaites and all who know them."

He drew the curtain, isolating them from the ballroom. "Why?"

Laughter caught in her throat. "It's a long story. And perhaps I am stupid after all."

"Stupid enough to let me take you into supper?"

He walked toward her, large, lithe, almost predatory. For some reason, her heartbeat quickened, not with fear or revulsion, but with excitement. She looked into his eyes as he crouched beside her chair, and again she felt that odd sense of drowning in familiarity, in a world where she truly wanted to be. Desire seeped into her bones, warm and thrilling. She wished he was Alan.

"Our carriage is ordered for midnight," she murmured. "Which is, perhaps, for the best."

"Why?" he asked again.

From some instinct she couldn't prevent, she lifted her hand and touched his cheek. Her fingertips glided from the silk of his mask to the warm, slightly rough skin of his jaw. Memory—or was it longing?—flooded her.

"Because I am grateful to you," she whispered, "and a little upset."

She let her hand fall, but he caught it in his.

"All the more reason to stay with me a little longer." He dropped a warm kiss in her palm.

Although she did not draw her hand free, she shook her head. "No. These things make me vulnerable," she said candidly. "And I think you know you already intrigue me too much."

"Too much for what?" he asked softly.

"Comfort. Which is why I have to go." She stood abruptly, but he rose with her, still holding her hand. and suddenly his lips were too close. A masked stranger she would never see again. One sweet, wicked kiss. Where would be the harm?

His breath hitched and quickened. His lips parted, descending closer yet.

"Thank you," she whispered and slid free.

Her hand on the curtain, she turned back to face him. He stood watching her, his face unreadable behind the mask.

"I won't forget what you did." She slipped around the curtain and walked quickly away, her heart thudding. She didn't know whether she felt more proud or regretful.

People were gathering and walking into supper. Across the ballroom, Ariadne waved to her and gestured toward the stairs.

It was time to go. Past time. Serena would look after Maria and the younger girls. The foreign officer, for whom she felt such an infinity was, in fact, a greater danger than the imbeciles on the terrace. He was temptation, even to a woman who loved her husband.

But she hated the sense of loss as she left him behind and hurried upstairs with Ariadne. It was as if her stupid emotions were already finding a replacement for Alan, as if she had already lost him. She refused to believe that. The eccentric stranger had been amusing, protective, and thoroughly capable. But he was not Alan.

The hired carriage was waiting for them at the front door. She and Ariadne climbed in and it set off.

"Another draw?" Ariadne asked her.

Frances smiled wearily. "Sadly, yes."

"Then we must find some other way to find a winner. Perhaps we should just both swagger about without disguises of any kind and see who calls one of us by the correct name first."

Frances tried to laugh, but was afraid she would cry instead. "I must be very tired," she whispered and closed her eyes. She wanted to see her baby. She wanted to go home to her husband.

OF COURSE, ARIADNE tried to talk her into staying. She had several amusing schemes, some of which even made Frances laugh as she took Jamie from Lawson. Apparently, Jamie had wakened more than an hour ago, crying inconsolably. Frances walked with him to her own chamber, saying, "I'll sleep on it, Ari, as should you. But I think I'm bored with this game."

"Very well." Ariadne wasn't pleased. There was a hint of ice in her voice, though that vanished when she added. "By the by, don't worry if you hear conversation in here later on. I am expecting a… guest."

Frances cast her a glance of half-impatient amusement. "A man? Did you make an assignation, Ari?"

"I might have. But don't worry. I'll kick him out before morning."

"You are a wicked woman," Frances drawled and closed the door.

Ari would tell her, she knew, that *she* should have made just such an assignation with the gentleman in the scarlet domino. But in truth, Frances only played at sophistication. Not through innate morality, but because until tonight, the only man she had ever wanted was Alan. And attraction, however sweet, just could not measure up to love.

She fell asleep with Jamie still in her arms, which was possibly why she woke at first light, a little stiff and uncomfortable. Jamie opened his eyes as she sat up, and smiled at her.

She smiled back. "Good morning, little man."

After feeding him, she washed and dressed them both quickly, and quietly left the chamber, carrying Jamie in her arms. Since a gentleman's somewhat worn coat lay over the back of the sofa, she assumed Ariadne's guest was still with her. Lawson stuck her head out of her own door.

"I'm just going for a walk," Frances told her. "I'll be back for breakfast."

"Very good, ma'am. Shall I take him?" Despite her initial disapproval of being used as a nurse, Lawson had quickly become one of Jamie's most devoted followers.

"No, thank you. I think the fresh air will do us both good."

It did. In a brisk walk up to the harbor and along the sand to

Blackhaven Cove, Jamie gurgled and smiled at everything. Gradually, the breeze seemed to blow the clouds of uncertainty from Frances's mind, and the sunshine to light her way. It would be difficult, but she knew exactly what she had to do.

"I'M GOING BACK to Torridon," Frances told Ariadne. She stood with her back to the window, while her friend sat on the sofa, her lips curved into a smile of vaguely contemptuous amusement. Ariadne's companion had left before Frances returned from her walk.

"I didn't know you had left him," Ariadne drawled.

"You know perfectly well I have not. I meant I am going back to Scotland, to Torridon House. No more wagers, no more silly games. I've already bespoken a vehicle for tomorrow morning, and I'm going to the castle this afternoon to call on my family." In particular, she needed to talk to Maria.

"I'm glad you have everything sorted out," Ariadne said, as though she did not care.

Frances took a step toward her. "What will you do?"

Ariadne shrugged. "Return to London, I suppose."

"Have you the means?" Frances asked bluntly.

Ariadne cast her a mocking glance. "My dear, I always have the means."

"We might come down for part of the season, I don't know. Or he might cast me off."

"For wagering the rubies?"

Frances smiled unhappily. "For taking our son and bolting. At least I did not *lose* the rubies."

"No. Actually…" Ariadne stood and paced around the room as though forcing herself to say or do something. "Actually, you won my diamonds."

Frances frowned. "I did? When?"

"Last night. Your brother called me Mrs. Marshall—quite politely, but he must have known perfectly well I was not invited."

"Then he knows I am here, too..."

"Why should you be? We do not come as an inevitable pair. He certainly did not mention you to me. And I kept quiet about it because I thought we could continue the wager. But..." A faint smile crossed her lips. "Play or pay. You won't play, so I must pay."

She went into her own chamber and emerged almost at once with her jewel case.

For Frances, there was no pleasure in winning. She knew well that the diamonds were one of the few valuable possessions Ari had left.

"We'll dine in the restaurant tonight," Frances said lightly. "Or in the castle if we are invited. And I shall wear your diamonds before returning them."

"You don't need to do that."

"It's only fair when we already agreed it for the rubies."

Ariadne regarded her with a hint of hauteur.

"The stakes were never equal since the rubies are not mine," Frances said. "The diamonds *are* yours."

"Actually, they're yours." Ariadne thrust the case into her hands.

"Until tomorrow." Frances closed her fingers around the box. "I shall enjoy wearing them—to say nothing of winning against you, for once."

Something flashed in Ariadne's eyes, an emotion Frances couldn't read. Her friend was too used to her own way, and yet she had nothing while Frances had everything... well, she had everything if Torridon ever forgave her for running away. And lying.

Banishing those thoughts, she took Ariadne's diamonds into her own bedchamber where Jamie slept. She knelt by the bed and pulled her portmanteau from underneath. Since she hadn't realized the rubies were in it when she left Torridon, it had seemed sensible to leave them there for safekeeping in the hotel. She thrust Ariadne's case inside, instinctively feeling for the other jewel case as she did so. Finding nothing, she peered impatiently inside.

Her heart lurched and seemed to stop. The case containing the ruby set was not there. Dropping the diamonds, she leapt to her feet, opening drawers and cupboards and frantically ransacking the few things within. She even crawled under the bed to see if the case had somehow fallen out of the portmanteau. In desperation, she wrenched open the diamond case, praying Ariadne was playing some trick on her. But no matter how hard she stared at the contents, the diamonds did not turn into rubies.

"Ari." She walked into the sitting room where Ariadne was putting on her bonnet to go out. "Ari, please tell me you've hidden the rubies, or that you're playing some other trick on me. I'll laugh, I promise."

"Don't be silly. You left them in your portmanteau, remember?"

"Yes, of course, I remember. But they're not there now! Oh, dear God, what do I do now? Lawson!"

The maid stuck her head out of Ariadne's chamber.

"You didn't move my jewel case for any reason, did you?" Frances asked hopefully.

"Oh no, my lady. I wouldn't touch your things," Lawson replied, affronted. "Not without your specific instruction."

"Of course you would not." Frances sank into the nearest chair, burying her face in her hands. "What am I going to do, Ari?"

"What you were going to do before. Go home and tell Torridon everything. If he loves you, he won't care."

"Won't care?" Frances repeated, raising her head to stare at her friends. "How can he love me, how can he believe I love him, when I have stolen his rubies! At best, I've lost the family heirloom; at worst, he'll think I've sold it to pay for our little jaunt! Can you really not see that this will confirm his worst suspicions? He will never believe me!"

Ariadne shrugged. "Then he isn't worth caring for. Give him my diamonds by way of compensation."

Frances closed her eyes, not unaware of her friend's generosity. "It isn't the same," she whispered. She pressed her knuckles to her burning cheeks. "They must have been stolen. Who could have done such a thing?"

"The chambermaid?" Ariadne said doubtfully. "Or any of the hotel staff, really. They could easily come in when we are all out."

"And be dismissed for stealing? Surely they would be the first suspects when I report this?"

"Yes, but any smart thief would already have got rid of them. They're too recognizable. He'll already have sold them on to someone who'll break them up."

"Sold them to whom?" Frances demanded. "Who in Blackhaven buys stolen goods?"

Even as she spoke the words, she knew how to find out. She knew the main haunt of the criminal fraternity. She even knew, suddenly, how to retrieve the rubies.

She jumped to her feet. "Lawson, go and bring the young porter here, will you?"

Lawson glanced in alarm at Ariadne, who jerked her head toward the door before going to Frances and seizing her by the wrist. "Wait, though. There is another suspect," she said reluctantly. "Another person was here, a man I do not know well enough to judge."

Frances's eyes widened. "Your companion of last night? Who was he?"

Ariadne drew in her breath. "Lord Sylvester Gaunt," she said ruefully. "Your sister's brother-in-law. He is wild to a fault and does not have the sweetest reputation. However, I'm sure he would not steal from family."

"Why not?" Frances said bleakly. "The other brother did, by all accounts. Besides, he wouldn't know I was family—unless you told him."

"Of course I didn't. I thought our wager was still on. Even though you had won."

Frances gave a shaky laugh. "It makes no difference, does it? Even if it was Gaunt, he would have sold it on, too. My one hope is that it hasn't yet left Blackhaven."

The door opened and Lawson returned with her most disapproving face, and the young porter. Frances smiled at him. She had picked on him for two reasons. He wasn't someone she knew from childhood, and he was about her own height. "Joe, isn't it? Do you live in here at the hotel?"

"Yes, ma'am…"

"Excellent. Then would you be so obliging as to lend me a set of your clothes?"

The boy's eyes darted helplessly around the room, as though searching for an ally. "I got nothing suitable, ma'am. Only my working clothes and the old, darned ones I wear when I clean the others."

"The old ones will be perfect. And I'll pay you enough for the loan of them that you can buy yourself a Sunday suit, too. But only if you keep this between us."

The boy shut his mouth. "Of course, ma'am," he said eagerly.

Chapter Seven

T HE ONLY FEMALES who frequented the tavern close to the market tended to be entirely unrespectable. Gillie Muir, now Lady Wickenden, had apparently once found her stepmother had taken a room there because it was cheap, and despite the quarrel between them at the time, had instantly brought her home. She had been so shocked, it had forced a reconciliation.

Certainly, it was not a place Frances would have dreamed of visiting had she not been desperate, but she knew all sorts of criminal types could be found there. In among the sailors, fishermen, and old soldiers, she knew there would be smugglers, thieves, fugitives and, no doubt, receivers of stolen goods.

Lady Torridon could not be seen in such a place. Even the widowed Mrs. Alan would have drawn far too much attention. And so, with a little help from the reluctant Ariadne, she dressed as a boy in Joe's old clothes, complete with a slightly greasy cap over her ruthlessly pinned hair.

"You look like a boy," Ari allowed, "albeit a very pretty boy. But you walk like a girl. Stride. Swagger. Also, try to speak lower, and your Scottish accent has to be much broader. You sound like the minister's wife rather than her gardener who ran away to sea."

"You are a hard task mistress," Frances said ruefully. "But quite right."

"I think we have to get another set of clothes so that I can come with you."

"Two such oddities will be too noticeable," Frances said. "On the other hand, I don't want to be murdered in there! If I don't come back in an hour, perhaps you could find an excuse to send in the watch?"

"You could be dead several times over in an hour," Ariadne said brutally. "Let us say half an hour."

"That barely gives me time to speak to anyone."

"Three quarters of an hour, then."

"One hour, Ari. Give me a chance."

"I'm trying. Are you sure this is the only way?"

"Unless you know how else to get the word out."

"I could ask Sylvester Gaunt."

"He's only been here two days and I will not involve Serena's brother-in-law!"

"Then why not send Joe rather than just using his clothes?"

"Because I can't tell him to go looking for stolen rubies, can I? Stop worrying. I'll be in and out again in no time."

"And if you're not, I'll send the watch," Ariadne agreed with obvious reluctance.

Frances shot her a cheeky grin and swaggered toward the door, where Lawson waited with Jamie. Frances kissed him, and Lawson checked the passage was clear before Frances slipped past her and bolted for the staff staircase which led down to the kitchens and the back door.

A minute later, she was striding up the high street.

It was one thing to plan this. It was quite another to shoulder her way between two sailors and a girl dressed in a low cut, ragged gown and, her heart thudding with anxiety, enter the den of iniquity.

If it hadn't been for the noise, she would have thought the taproom was closed, for at first, she couldn't see anyone in it. Tobacco smoke hung like fog in the air, stinging her eyes, blinding her. The stench of stale sweat and old beer almost choked her. She froze just inside the door, wishing she hadn't been so stupid as to come here.

But there was no other choice. As her eyes grew more used to the gloom, she made out a counter and a villainous looking individual behind it. She moved toward it, though there was not enough space to stride let alone swagger. No one got out of her way, but on the other hand, no one paid her much attention either.

The man behind the counter, no doubt the landlord, was listening to the man seated on the other side of it. Frances couldn't understand a word. But she knew instinctively it would not do to show anxiety or fear in a place like this. Having waited a few moments to be noticed, she interrupted.

"Ale, if you please," she growled hoarsely.

The landlord looked at her while his other customer carried on talking. She slapped her hand on the wet, sticky counter, doubly glad of Joe's woolen gloves which she'd worn only to hide her soft, white hands.

The landlord reached up and brought down a mug from the shelf above. It didn't look terribly clean but he slopped some ale into it and held out his hand for payment. Frances lifted her hand revealing the sovereign beneath, like a ship about to sink into the murky sea of spilled ale and spirits on the counter.

The landlord raised his eyes from the sovereign to her face.

"I don't want change," she uttered in an accent Glasgow thieves would have been proud of. "If you help me out. I'm looking to buy some jewelry."

"There's a shop in High Street."

Frances gave him what she hoped was a cheeky grin. "Cannae afford they prices. If you see what I mean."

"You're twelve years old," the landlord retorted. "You can't afford any prices." All the same, he swept up the sovereign.

"I'm not," she said. "And I can. I'll be sitting over there if you come across someone wanting to sell."

With that, she swiped up the heavy mug and took it to a small empty table where she forced herself down on a chair that made her skin crawl. She hadn't expected to be quite so physically repelled by the place. Her main worry had been its patrons, most of whom, according to Gervaise, would cut their own grandmother's throats for a shilling. But in fact, singly and in groups, the customers didn't pay much attention to each other. A question, she supposed, of seeing no evil and hearing no evil. And having the same courtesy extended to oneself. It was honor of a sort. If it worked, which she doubted.

She did her best to sprawl, and forced herself to drink some ale, which was pretty disgusting. She pretended to take bigger draughts than she did and wiped the back of her glove over her mouth.

Someone slid onto the stool opposite, a wiry man with darting eyes. "I hear you're looking for jewelry."

"If it's the right quality and the right price. What have you got?"

The man laid his fist on the table and opened his fingers very briefly to reveal an emerald ring and what looked like a bracelet set with diamonds and sapphires.

"I'm looking for rubies," Frances said.

"I can get you rubies."

"When?"

The man thought about it. "A week, maybe."

"Too long. But thanks."

The man shrugged and stood up. "Please yourself."

Surreptitiously, she glanced at the timepiece hidden in Joe's coat pocket. It had already been half an hour since she had left the hotel. She began to realize that this would not be a quick quest. But she could not stay here all day. Ariadne would send the watch. And she needed to feed Jamie.

She waited another quarter hour, thinking deeply, but no one approached her. Dissatisfied, she rose and walked back up to the counter.

"I'll come back tomorrow morning at ten," she told the landlord gruffly. "There's another sovereign for you if you arrange a meeting with anyone who has what I want." She looked him in the eye. "I like rubies."

The landlord just stared at her. But there was nothing else she could do. She made her way through the fog of smoke to the door. Just as she raised her hand to it, it opened. And she looked up into the face of her husband.

SHE RECOGNIZED HIM this time without any difficulty. Even through the gloom of the taproom, he saw her eyes widen with undisguised horror, and the blood drain from her face, leaving it white and sick.

It wasn't the reaction he'd hoped to inspire in his wife when they met again. But then, it had never entered his head that he would meet her at all in such an establishment, let alone dressed like a street urchin in boys' clothes. He had only come in for a change of scene and a mug of ale to help him think and plan his next move.

But one could never predict Frances, and she had made the move for him.

After the first stunned instant, rage overwhelmed him, fed largely by fear for her. And, if he was honest, by that expression of horror in her face. Never had he thought to find such a look directed at him. Not from her.

He wrenched his gaze from her face to the table by the door. His stare must have been ferocious for the fishermen there shuffled up the bench to the next table.

"Sit," he snarled at his wife, who stepped back and dropped onto the stool as though he had struck her. He slid onto the bench opposite and leaned across the table. "What in God's name are you doing in this place?"

"I didn't know you were in Blackhaven," she blurted. "I didn't know."

"That, madam, is patently obvious. I ask again, what are you doing here?"

A thousand expressions seemed to chase each other across her eyes, before her lashes swept down, veiling them. And when she raised them again, he could read nothing except a certain desperation that she couldn't quite hide.

"A wager," she said.

He curled his lip. "With Ariadne Marshall?" When she nodded, he looked around him in exaggerated expectation. "And yet I don't see her here."

"Of course you don't. But she'll send the watch if I'm not back in ten minutes. I have to go."

At least she had taken that much care. But his blood still ran cold when he thought what could have happened to her in this place. She made to rise, but he shot out his hand and seized her wrist. She stilled, gazing not at his face but at his detaining fingers.

"What did you wager?"

She shrugged. "Ari's diamonds. I've won them for a night." She swallowed. "Let me go, Alan. I'll come up to the castle tomorrow and tell everyone everything. And I'll do whatever you want."

He released her as though she'd stung him. *I'll do whatever you want.* A submission, a sacrifice to his undoubted rights. He wanted to drag her back right now. He wanted to push her away and never see her again, only his heart would crumble into a million pieces. It was already cracking.

She jumped up with painful relief and bolted out the door. He rose and followed, to be sure no one impeded her. By the time he reached the step, she was running up the road to High Street, fast. She didn't run like a boy.

Torridon backed inside and sat staring at the table.

A wiry man slid onto the stool Frances had just vacated. His eyes darted around the room. "Got any jewelry to sell, your worship?"

"My worship? I've never been called that before. And no, why would you imagine I did?"

"Young shaver there is keen to buy rubies. But I'll take anything. Or if you want to buy—"

"I don't want to buy or sell," Torridon interrupted, staring at him. *Desperate to buy rubies.* In this place, stolen rubies. It all began to make sense to him. Sort of.

His companion sloped away again. After a minute or two, Torridon stood and walked over to the counter. Feeling the need of it, he ordered brandy instead of ale.

"Young lad who just left," he said to the landlord, who made no sign he knew who Torridon was talking about. "I might have something for him. Do you know where I can reach him?"

The landlord shrugged. "He said he'd be in tomorrow morning at ten."

Torridon smiled grimly.

FRANCES FLED THROUGH the hotel kitchen and up the back stairs, desperate to reach the safety of her rooms. She was almost at the landing when one of the clerks shouted down. "You there, where do you think you are going? Come here!"

Frances bolted up the last few steps, through the passage door, then all but fell into her own room, closing the door behind her as softly as she could before sliding her back down it to sit on the floor.

Ariadne gawped at her. Frances put her finger to her lips.

"Thank God," Ariadne murmured, paying that little attention. "Did someone see you?"

From the passage came the sound of someone panting, then footsteps scurrying along the corridor toward the main stairs.

"Yes, but he's gone."

"Then we are in the clear."

"Not by a long chalk. We are quite in the basket now." Frances hauled herself from the floor and went through to her bedchamber, where Jamie was sleeping peacefully. She came back and threw herself onto the sofa beside Ariadne.

"Didn't you find a trace of the rubies?" Ariadne asked sympathetically.

"No, not yet, but I did find my husband!"

Alarm surged into Ariadne's face before she had time to smooth it away. "Oh dear. Did he recognize you?"

"Oh, yes. And oh, Ari, he was so angry."

"I expect he was," Ari said with a trace of humor. "I don't care for the man, but be reasonable, my love. *Any* husband is unlikely to be conciliatory having found his wife in a dangerous tavern dressed as a boy."

Frances gave a choke of laughter that was close to tears. "You are right, of course."

"I suppose he is on his way here?"

"Oh God, I hope not!" She frowned. "No, he can't be. He might guess where we're staying, but he can't know. And I doubt he would risk scandal by asking for me here. I said I would see him at the castle tomorrow. If I haven't found the rubies by then, I'll just have to tell him everything without the sop of his returned heirloom."

"So you didn't tell him the rubies were stolen?"

"God, no. I doubt he knows I took them with me from home. But I've left word at the tavern for anyone who has rubies to sell to meet me there tomorrow morning. Hopefully, I will have them back by the time I go the castle."

"Pertinent question, Frannie. What are you planning to use to buy back the rubies? I understand that you won't need to pay anything like their true value. But I still doubt whatever is left of your pin money will be enough."

Frances hit her forehead. "I am an imbecile! I so rarely pay for anything over the counter... but a thief is unlikely to send me a bill!"

"Or Torridon to pay it, if he did," Ariadne interjected.

"Oh the *devil*, just when I thought I might get clear..." Frances buried her face in her hands.

Ariadne put an arm around her. "Fear not, my dear, we still have the diamonds. Sell them. Swap them."

Frances lifted her head. "Oh, Ari, I couldn't, not just to buy what I allowed to be stolen."

"Why not?" Ariadne said brightly. "You would do the same for me. And it isn't really about the rubies, is it? It's about your marriage."

Frances gave a twisted smile. "It is important to me. He is important to me."

"I know. Though I have said it before and I'll say it again, he does not deserve you."

"No, he doesn't," Frances agreed, though for different reasons entirely. She sprang up. "I had better change out of these clothes and ask Joe if I can keep them until tomorrow."

Ten minutes later as she returned to the sitting room in her morning dress, carrying Jamie, she said impulsively, "Ari, do you think Russians are wealthy?"

Ariadne laughed. "What an odd question! Of course, some of them will be rich. I believe the nobility live in huge palaces—well the ones Bonaparte did not destroy. Moscow was burned to the ground, was it not?"

Ignoring the question, Frances said, "Would you mind if I used your diamonds as security against a loan from a friend?"

"I've already said, use them as you wish," Ariadne replied. There was nothing in her face and voice to show she disapproved, but Frances, morbidly sensitive, was afraid she didn't like the idea.

"You know I will move heaven and earth to get them back for you."

She shrugged, lazy amusement seeping from her eyes. "They are yours, Frannie."

"For one night. I have hopes it will be no more. May I borrow Lawson to carry a message to the castle?"

"You may borrow her to *dance* at the castle if such is your desire," Ariadne drawled.

Frances giggled, her good humor restored by a plan that might just work. With Jamie on her knee, she sat at the desk and wrote a short note which she folded and sealed while Lawson waited patiently at her shoulder.

"I would like you to take this up to the castle," she said, "and deliver it to the Russian gentleman who is staying there. That is, I think he is Russian, but he is certainly foreign. He is tall and dark and amusing, and he wore a scarlet domino to the ball. You must only give this into his hands, and discreetly. If necessary, tell Mrs. Gaskell the housekeeper – in private – that it is from Lady Frances, and she will help you. But no one else is to know anything about me or this message."

"I am a lady's maid, my lady," Lawson uttered, affronted. "Not a messenger boy."

"I know," Frances replied steadily. "I am asking you as a favor, not giving you an instruction."

Lawson glanced at Ariadne who was studiously reading. Perhaps it entered her head that her current mistress was in financial difficulties and might not be paying her for much longer. Or perhaps she was persuaded by her love for Jamie. Whatever her reasons, though she sniffed, she took the letter, seized her shawl from her own chamber, and departed.

MRS. GASKELL HAD been housekeeper at Braithwaite Castle since the current earl's father had brought home his bride. Devoted to the family, she missed Lady Frances since her marriage, and found her eyes misting whenever she thought of Lady Serena's imminent departure with her husband to Devon. She had helped both of them out of childish scrapes in the past, and told them off for them, too. So, when Harry the footman first came to her and said a maid had arrived with a message for a Russian gentleman, she suspected Serena had been up to mischief at the ball.

"Thing is," Harry explained, bearding her in the housekeeper's room along the passage from the kitchen, "we told her there's no foreign gent staying here, but she won't go away and insists on seeing you."

Mrs. Gaskell couldn't help liking the idea that the young ladies still relied on her. "Bring her here, then Harry, and I'll deal with her."

Harry beckoned toward the door and a very respectable, stern looking lady's maid entered as Harry went out.

The maid approached her, clutching an epistle in her hand. "I have a message from Lady Frances," she said, a trifle grimly.

Mrs. Gaskell raised her eyebrows in astonishment. "Lady *Frances*?

Not Lady Serena?"

"Lady Frances."

"Well!" Mrs. Gaskell frowned. "I am at a loss. There is no foreign gentleman currently staying at the castle. And we are not expecting any more guests. Even the family are preparing to leave. Is Lady Frances quite well?"

"Quite. The gentleman is tall and dark," the maid said, as though repeating a lesson. "And amusing. Apparently. And he wore a scarlet domino to the ball."

Mrs. Gaskell's jaw dropped. And then she laughed. She remembered quite well who had worn the scarlet domino. "Bless them." Pulling herself together, she held out the hand for the note. "Thank you. I know now whom she means. I shall give it to him directly."

But the woman snatched the letter back. "If you please, ma'am, her ladyship was quite particular that I should deliver it only to the gentleman. Discreetly."

More intrigued than angry, Mrs. Gaskell nevertheless drew herself up to her full, not very considerable height. "My good woman, you must take my word that a strange maid chasing around the castle after this particular gentleman would cause just the sort of talk her ladyship would most dislike. You are clearly aware her ladyship trusts me. *I* will give the letter discreetly to the gentleman."

The maid hesitated, then shrugged as if she had had enough of the whole affair, and thrust the letter at Mrs. Gaskell, who hid it immediately in the folds of her gown. Having shown the maid out again, she told Harry there had clearly been a misunderstanding, and sent him back upstairs to his duties.

Mrs. Gaskell was aware that Lord Torridon had gone out early. She worried that he looked so moody and tempestuous. She worried even more that Lady Frances was not with him. At least the family did not seem remotely anxious. They said Lord Torridon was merely stopping over on his way south. Which was reasonable. And it was equally reasonable that Lady Frances should write to her husband. Only why the secrecy and the strange maid? And why call him foreign?

He was Scottish, of course, and not English, but one didn't normally call Scots foreigners, and how it got muddled into Russian was quite beyond her.

She went about her upstairs duties, choosing those that took her to areas around the front hall. She was arranging fresh spring flowers at various points when Lord Torridon was finally admitted. While he gave up his coat and hat, she walked toward the staircase, reaching it at much the same time he did.

"Good afternoon, my lord."

He nodded curtly, but gestured her to precede him. She did so, but having checked there was no one else on the stairs who could see them, she fell back to ascend beside him, and held out the letter.

"This was delivered by hand," she murmured. "It purports to come from Lady Torridon."

His gaze flew to her face, then dropped to the letter, which he quickly took and pocketed. "Does it, by God? Thank you."

"If I can be of assistance," Mrs. Gaskell said delicately, "please call on me." And she hurried on upstairs.

IMPATIENTLY, TORRIDON FLUNG into his own bedchamber and dismissed his valet before tearing the seal on the letter and sinking down on the bed to read it. He didn't know quite what he expected, Some explanation, perhaps, for her bizarre, dangerous, behavior. A request to come home, perhaps. Even – his heart beat harder at the thought – a word of love.

But it was quite other.

My dear sir,

I am the lady to whom you provided such kind assistance at the recent ball. I have no right to call upon you for further help. Only my belief that you offered such with sincerity, and my conviction that you are worthy of a lady's trust, has convinced me to write to you now.

I am in the sad position, through my own foolishness and care-

lessness, of needing to conduct a not entirely reputable piece of business. As such, I humbly request to draw upon your protection and your funds. If you have access to a sum of approximately five hundred pounds, I believe that would answer. I can provide you with security until I pay the money back. If you are able and willing to help, please meet me at the Blackhaven Tavern at ten of the clock tomorrow morning and I shall explain all. In the meantime, I can be reached at the Blackhaven Hotel, under the name of Mrs. Alan, if you would be so good as to reply.

However, please be assured that if you find yourself unable to help in this case, for whatever reasons, I shall remain your grateful if desperate friend,

The Lady in Blue.

P.S. If you come to the tavern, I shall not look as you expect.

Torridon's lips twitched at the last line. How was it, however much she infuriated or bewildered him, she always made him laugh?

Clearly the letter was not written to her husband, whatever Mrs. Gaskell imagined, or how she had come to that conclusion. The letter was to the Russian stranger who had danced with her at the ball and beaten off the drunken louts who appeared to have threatened her mischievous little sisters before she had defended them.

She was magnificent in her own way. But now, what the devil was she about? What could she want with five hundred pounds at the tavern? Except to buy stolen goods. The rubies she had been so interested in. He was right. The rubies *had* been stolen and she was desperate to find them and buy them back before he discovered their loss. So desperate that she risked herself at the tavern and tried to borrow money from a stranger.

She must be very frightened of him. Guilt smote him. Had he been so fierce, so unkind that she was truly afraid of him? So afraid that she would run away from him, and turn to another man for help rather than to her own husband?

It crushed him that she should feel this way. But Frances was not a fearful person. There was more to this than avoiding confrontation with a stern husband. She had already said she would come to the castle tomorrow and tell everything.

He let the letter fall from his fingers, wondering how she could have lost the rubies in the first place, who could possibly have stolen them. She had told him she'd gone to the tavern for a wager, for Ariadne Marshall's diamonds. That had obviously been a lie, but still, he suspected the diamonds were involved—as security perhaps, for the five hundred pounds with which she wanted to buy back the stolen rubies.

She couldn't be aware the diamonds were no use as security. Torridon happened to know they were paste, because Ariadne had sold the real set years ago to bail Tom Marshall out of debt.

Abruptly, the puzzle clicked into place in his mind. He knew who had taken the rubies.

Chapter Eight

OR THE FIRST time ever, Maria was not looking forward to her secret assignation with Gideon. She would never have believed he could turn into the slurring, staggering fool she had encountered on the terrace the previous night, a man, moreover, who had done nothing to protect her or her little sisters from his even drunker friends. That had been undertaken by a female stranger. Or at least, so Maria hoped. Her sisters were divided on the issue.

"I'm sure it was Frances," Alice said stubbornly when they were discussing the matter in her bedchamber.

"Frances isn't here," Maria said tiredly. She was torn between wishing for her eldest sister to confide in and advise her, and praying she was nowhere near and would never know Maria's folly.

"I think we just *want* it to be Frances," Helen said ruefully. "So long as she doesn't tell Mama."

"Well, she told Serena," Alice pointed out. "Although that is a lot better than Mama."

Devastated by such an unpleasant outcome to her first romance, Maria contemplated simply hiding in the castle until they left for London with Mama next week. She had no need, and at this moment no desire, to speak to Lieutenant Heath again. She rather wanted him to wait for her and suffer her absence, and finally understand that he had ruined everything.

On the other hand, it might make him reckless enough to come to the castle. And she knew in her heart she had to end this cleanly and in person.

She stood abruptly. "I'm going for a walk."

"I'll come with you," Helen said at once.

"No, not this time," Maria said firmly. "I need to be alone."

Helen sniffed. As Maria left the room, determined to get the unpleasant business over with, she heard Helen say, "She's gone to meet that lieutenant again."

"Of course she has," Alice said scornfully.

So much for secrecy.

With the hood of her cloak pulled up over her hair, she slipped out of the castle though the side entrance Serena used to use to meet Tamar before they were married. She had thought no one knew they trysted in the orchard. Maria was wiser. She hurried through the wooded land at the back of the castle, following the path until she reached the dead elm tree near the road to the Black Fort.

For the first time ever, her heart sank when she saw Gideon pacing back and forth across the path. He stopped as soon as he heard her and came to meet her, not with his usual impetuous stride, but more slowly, almost apologetically. His face was pale, his jaw slightly discolored, and his eyes blood-shot. He did not look well, and in spite of her anger, she felt sorry for him.

"Maria," he uttered. "I didn't think you would come."

"I almost didn't," she admitted. "But I owe it to you to meet in person."

He closed his eyes. "Don't, Maria. Please, don't."

She swallowed. "Don't what?" she said, with unnecessary aggression.

"Throw me over. Hate me." He opened his eyes and took a step nearer, though he didn't try to touch her. "I am so sorry. I let you down and behaved abominably. In your brother's home, too. To be honest, it's all a bit of a blur. I had far too much brandy. And wine." He smiled hesitantly. "It was Dutch courage, you see. I was going to speak to your brother about us, only once I was bosky, I forgot the purpose of it."

"Just as well," Maria said. "I can just imagine Braithwaite's face if you weaved up to him, slurring my name and breathing brandy fumes all over him!"

Gideon flinched. "It doesn't bear thinking of." He rubbed his jaw. "Someone hit me. I think it sobered me up because I left after that. You wouldn't believe my head today."

"It serves you right."

"Yes, it does," he agreed. "And I want you to know that I will never drink again." He did take her hand now, and in spite of all her intentions, she let him. "Forgive me?" he begged.

"I'm not sure I do," she said honestly. "Apart from anything else, it isn't fun anymore, sneaking about and lying. Even my little sisters know I'm lying, and if Serena gets wind of my meeting you, if Gervaise does, or my mother..." She shuddered. "Last night opened my eyes, Gideon. To many things. I don't want us to meet anymore."

A desperate look came into his eyes. "Don't say that. But I agree, this sneaking doesn't suit either of us. Very well, let us simply get married."

Maria blinked. "I am only just sixteen years old. Neither Gervaise nor my mother will allow it."

"Then we present them with a *fait accompli*." His slightly red eyes shining now, he grinned at her. "Scotland is not far away. Let us elope!"

To PLEASE ARIADNE, Frances wore the diamonds that evening and went downstairs with her to dine in the hotel dining room. She wore her veil to walk to the discreet table they had bespoken, though she lifted it once they were seated.

"There isn't much point in hiding anymore," she said ruefully. "Tomorrow, everyone will know."

Ariadne shrugged. "I doubt they'll ever connect Mrs. Alan with Lady Torridon. In fact, I almost wish we were still wagering, to see if anyone knows you now. I'd wager not. For what it's worth."

Frances regarded her tolerantly. "You are indefatigable, Ari."

"I am, but I do blame myself for the loss of the rubies—"

"Hush," Frances interrupted, fingering the sparkling stones at her throat. "We will not talk of that tonight, if you please, I am enjoying the fruits of our last wager."

They ate a most pleasant meal and laughed together over previous adventures and old gossip. Frances almost forgot the lead weight in her stomach caused by the loss of the rubies. She tried not to imagine Torridon's face when she told him what had happened. But she still had hope. Even if the Russian let her down, she would still go to the tavern tomorrow morning and give everything she had for the rubies' return. Perhaps if she threatened the thief with the magistrate, he would hand them over for a pittance...

"So," Ariadne said, interrupting her train of thought, "who is this Russian you sent for?"

"Someone who did me a kindness at the ball," she said as negligently as she could.

"Not the one who scared off the drunk intruders?"

"Yes, as it happens."

"So, you are rewarding him for rescuing you, with the honor of another opportunity?"

Frances gave a crooked smile. "Something like that."

"Not sure it works that way, but I admire your spirit. Will he give you the money?"

"I don't know. I told you, I offered your diamonds as security, but I have no idea what his circumstances are. To be honest, I was hoping to hear from him before now."

"Well, even if he doesn't have the kind of money you need, he can at least be your bodyguard in that place!"

"I think he would be good at that," Frances said, brightening, "and it shouldn't be *too* full of violent thieves at ten in the morning, should it?"

"Of course not. In fact, if you—and he—play your cards well, I wouldn't be surprised if you retrieved the rubies for nothing. I wish I could help more."

"Trust me, the diamonds are invaluable in this," Frances assured her. "And if the worst comes, I can always make an appointment at Jenner's Bank and withdraw funds in my own name. Only, people would talk when Torridon is here and I am reluctant to inflict even more scandal upon him. Especially if no one brings me the rubies."

"Frannie, you worry too much," Ariadne told her, reaching for her wine glass. "You have a wealthy husband and a home, and what's more, a devoted family to fall back on if Himself needs time to come around. Nothing bad will come from this." She lifted the wine glass in a silent toast. "To your Russian, with whom you should enjoy a night of passion before returning to your dull but wealthy husband."

"Torridon is not remotely dull!" Frances protested, ignoring the rest of the speech.

"I know he is not, but it is such fun to make you defend him."

Frances smiled reluctantly, raised her glass and then drank.

"You do know," Ariadne said, lowering her glass again, "that you put several noses out of joint when you snagged Torridon."

Frances laughed. She wasn't quite as naïve as Ariadne imagined. "I couldn't believe my luck when he offered for *me*," she confided. "Not with all the other lures being cast out to him. And it was what my mother and Braithwaite wanted, too."

"Fortunately, it was also what Torridon and his mother wanted."

Francis frowned, pushing her plate aside, "What do you mean?"

"I mean it was a good match. For both families."

She hadn't done it for her family. Oh, she had been glad the match pleased them, but it wasn't why she had accepted. She had been ridiculously in love with Torridon from the first time she'd looked up into his smiling eyes. She had adored that those eyes could dance while his lips remained grave and polite, as though, like her, he found so much of fashionable life amusing in ways no one else comprehended.

Ariadne did not understand... or did she? Was she warning Frances of the reality she had been trying not to see? That however much Frances loved her husband, Torridon had merely made a good match for the benefit of his name and his family.

"Shall we have desserts?" Ariadne asked.

"Of course." Frances pulled herself together to speak to the waiter now hovering beside them. As she did so, she became aware that Ariadne's gaze was fixed on something or someone in the dining room. Her gaze flickered to Frances with a tiny, warning frown.

Every hair on Frances's neck stood up. Alarm, awareness, a silly surge of elation. She knew who it was before he spoke.

"Good evening, ladies. What a pleasant surprise," Torridon said ironically.

His voice seemed to reach deep inside her, turn her outside in. What was he doing here? Had he somehow got wind of her message to the Russian? They were staying under the same roof... unless the Russian had already left Blackhaven. But if Alan had got the note, what in God's name would he think? In sheer panic, she held herself rigid, unable even to turn to face him. It was he who moved, brushing past her chair to stand between her and Ariadne.

"The pleasure is all ours," Ariadne drawled. "How do you do, Torridon?"

"How do *you* do, Mrs. Marshall?" he returned politely.

"You are just in time for desserts," Ariadne told him. "Do join us."

Frances flicked her eyes up at him, both dreading and longing for his company.

Torridon met her gaze, his own unreadable. She had no idea why he had come, if he knew of her note or not. "Oh, no," he replied evenly. His gaze flickered to the diamonds at her throat. "I am only passing. I shall not intrude. And how is our son?"

"He's with Lawson," Frances blurted, feeling unaccountably guilty. "He's fine."

A sardonic, cold little smile touched his lips. "And since I can see you are both in excellent health, too, my evening is complete. Mrs. Marshall. Frances." He bowed to each of them in turn.

He was going to leave again already, just as if they really were strangers. Outrage blended with her panic and almost without meaning to, she flung out her hand to his.

For an instant, surprise flickered in his eyes. He took her hand, his strong fingers warm and rough in texture, although his grip was gentle. He bowed again, brushing his lips across her knuckles. Her breath caught on a rush of tingling warmth.

"Until tomorrow," he said deliberately and, releasing her hand, he walked away leaving her bereft and cold.

ALTHOUGH SHE ASKED on her way back to their rooms, no messages had been left for her. Nor had Lawson taken charge of any. The maid swore she had given the note to Mrs. Gaskell, and that Mrs. Gaskell had known whom she meant. It seemed Frances was on her own. But at least it seemed to be mere coincidence that Torridon had appeared at the hotel. He couldn't have known of her plea to the Russian.

Well, she would return to the tavern in the morning in her male clothing, with or without the Russian, and if she found the rubies, she would simply strike as good a bargain as she could, and draw on the bank in her husband's name to buy them back. It would be safer than threatening the thief with the magistrate. And she could not drag the authorities with her to the tavern. She shuddered at the scandal that would cause.

She sighed as she laid Jamie down to sleep after his last feed of the day. She very much doubted there would ever be a funny side of this affair to laugh over with Torridon.

She climbed into bed and blew out the candle. Whatever happened about the rubies, tomorrow would be a difficult day. But there would be some relief in honest confession. And pleasure in seeing her family, even if Torridon shunned her.

Her busy brain would not allow her to fall asleep for some time, but eventually the darkness closed in around her and she dropped into an uneasy slumber.

She woke, disoriented but with the certain knowledge that someone was in the chamber with her. And it couldn't be Alan, she grasped, finally, because she was in the hotel.

"Ari?" she whispered, "Is that you?"

"No," came back a deeper voice than she expected. Closer than she expected, too. From instinct, she slid out of bed on the side farthest from the voice and closest to the cradle. "Don't be frightened. It is I." The whisper rose to a low, husky sound with a distinctly Russian accent.

"You?" she uttered, peering into the darkness.

"Didn't you send for me?"

"Not to come to my bedchamber in the middle of the night," she whispered furiously. "How did you get in?"

"The outer door was not locked."

"Not...!" But of course, Ariadne would be out trysting with her new lover, and Lawson, waiting up for her, would not consider locking the door. Even though it seemed anyone could walk in without her knowing. "She doesn't know, does she?" Frances asked uneasily.

"Who?"

"Lawson! The maid."

"Of course not. I am most discreet. Come back into bed before you catch cold."

The words sounded so intimate that she blushed in the covering darkness. "I hope you are standing decorously on the other side of it."

The bed creaked as he stood up. "Of course, I am."

She didn't know whether to laugh or order him out. While she decided, she climbed into bed and pulled the covers up to her chin. "I didn't send for you, you know. I merely asked if you could help."

"Well, since you told me where you were, I chose to reply in person. What exactly is your problem, madam?"

"Wait, let me light the candle." She reached for the flint on the bedside table, but his fingers closed around her wrist, not rough but certainly immovable.

"No," he warned. "I think our business is best conducted in the dark."

She frowned, although he wouldn't be able to see it. "What do you mean by that?"

"That I doubt you want to be discovered by this Lawson of yours. Or 'Ari.'"

"Oh." Hastily, she told him the story in bare terms, without detail, about quarreling with her husband, bolting to Edinburgh with the rubies accidentally in her portmanteau, and how she and her friend had made a wager that they would not be recognized by their respective families if they chose not to be. And how she had eventually won the wager but discovered the rubies to have been stolen.

"And you are convinced you will find them at the tavern?" the Russian asked doubtfully.

"It's the only place I know likely to handle stolen goods," she confided. "And surely the thief would want to be rid of them quickly?"

"Yes, but I imagine he might go to Carlisle—or even to Whalen— to find a better buyer. For such fine jewels as you describe, it would even be worth his while to take them directly to London. Or abroad."

"Oh." Crestfallen, she let her shoulders droop.

He covered her hands with his. Only then did she realize he was perched comfortably on the bed beside her. "I'm only warning of the worst, in case you are disappointed."

"So, would you lend me the money? And come with me tomorrow, to look out for me?"

"No," he said.

She swallowed her disappointment, merely attempting to draw her hands free.

He held onto them. "I will not come with you," he repeated. "I will go in your stead and pay what is necessary."

"As a loan?" she said, insistent even in her desperate state that there should be no misunderstanding.

"If you wish."

"I do."

He was silent a moment, then said, "I don't wish to speak out of turn, but will you not apply to your husband for funds to pay me back? In which case, it would be simpler just to tell him everything now."

"Oh no, I plan to pay you back from my pin money," she assured him. "I hope you don't mind that it will take a few months."

"Years, I should think."

"Oh no, I'm sure we needn't pay the rubies' full value to a thief," she said blithely, "and my husband is most generous in that way."

"I see." She could not see his eyes in the darkness, but she was sure they were fixed on her face. "In what ways, then, is your husband not generous?"

"None," she said at once. "He is generous to a fault in all things."

"Then why are you so afraid to tell him?"

She leaned forward impulsively. "Oh, can't you see how it looks? I ran off without a word to him, taking the rubies. And the next he hears about it, I tell him they were stolen from me! I'm not *afraid* to tell him. I just want to do so once I have them safely back. It will be so much more comfortable for both of us..." She trailed off, as her reasoning didn't seem to work so well when spoken aloud.

"Whatever you wish," he said. Unexpectedly, something brushed lightly, warmly against her cheek, surely his fingers. "Either way, I will help you."

She caught his hand and squeezed it. "Thank you," she said and released him. "And now, you must go."

There was a pause. "Must I?"

She couldn't help smiling. "Yes," she said firmly.

The mattress shifted again as he stood. "Until tomorrow." There was only the faintest sound of movement as he approached the bedchamber door.

In sudden alarm, she bolted out of bed, rushing after the blacker shadow, almost knocking against Jamie's cradle in her haste. "Wait!"

She bumped into something solid—the Russian—and clutched his arms to steady herself. "What if Lawson is there? Let me look—"

But she could not go anywhere. His arms were around her, holding her against his hard, lean body. His breath on her lips gave her an instant's warning. Her heart lurched in panic and then his mouth fell on hers, crushing her lips, opening them before she could object.

His hand cupped her cheek, brushed her neck before settling at her nape, holding her head steady for his kiss. He gentled it, perhaps afraid of frightening her, caressed her lips more tenderly, his tongue sensual yet undemanding as it stroked hers.

But she wasn't afraid at all. Her mouth, her whole body thrilled to his touch, ached for more. She could not let herself respond. There was betrayal enough in not throwing him off.

"Enough," she whispered against his lips. "I will not do this."

His lips fastened more strongly, making her gasp, but only for a moment before he raised his head and released her. "It was never a condition of my help," he said huskily. The door opened and closed so quickly that the light from the single candle in the sitting room barely reached her.

She held her breath, waiting for Lawson's scream that never came.

Eventually, when her straining ears picked up nothing more, she felt her way back to bed. Thank God Jamie had slept through everything. For a while she lay awake, her fingers on her lips. No man but Alan had ever kissed her mouth. She wished it hadn't been quite so exciting... the familiarity of such a tender embrace mingled with the novelty of a wilder sensuality, so hard to resist.

She squeezed her eyes shut. She missed Alan. She wanted the Russian to have been Alan.

Chapter Nine

O N FIRST WAKING, Frances felt much more comfortable than she
had the evening before. The Russian was taking care of any
transaction in the tavern and would do so with much more skill and
authority over such company than she could ever manage.

Only, as she fed Jamie, she wondered if that were true. She was
trusting a man she barely knew, because he had once done her a good
turn. Or because he flattered her wounded heart. But would an
honorable man kiss a woman he knew to be married? Admittedly, he
had pushed it no further and had certainly not made it a condition of
his aid, but still, in the cold light of day, this made her uneasy. And she
was trusting him with the rubies which were her husband's.

Since leaving Torridon House that morning—it seemed a lifetime
ago—she had been making bad decisions and worse decisions. Her
instinct might be to trust the Russian, but instinct had led her away
from Torridon and into the increasingly crazy wagers with Ariadne.
She should have sent the rubies home with the coach from Edinburgh...

It was no use crying over spilt milk. She could not alter what she
had done, but she could stop acting foolishly. She should not, could
not leave this transaction solely up to the Russian. She needed him to
protect her as he had already shown he could do. But she had to see
and handle the rubies herself... if they were indeed there to be
retrieved.

Lawson obligingly went to fetch her coffee, without being asked.
By the time the maid returned, she stood in the sitting room, cram-

ming her hair under Joe the porter's cap. Jamie lay on a blanket by the sofa, gurgling happily.

Lawson set the coffee down on the table, her lips thin with disapproval. "Not again."

"One more time." Frances picked up the cup of coffee and drank gratefully. "There's no need to wake Mrs. Marshall if she was home late."

Lawson sniffed. Clearly, she disapproved of her mistress, too.

"Will you watch over Jamie for me?" Frances asked. "I should be back in an hour, hopefully less."

"'Course I will," Lawson said, her stern face breaking into smiles in response to Jamie's.

"Thank you, Lawson," Frances said warmly. "I don't know what I would have done without you this last week."

As before, she slipped out through the busy kitchen without greater notice than a cook shouting at her for getting under her feet. With the cap low over her eyes, and her hands shoved inside the pockets of the baggy coat that disguised her shape, she swaggered up High Street and turned right toward the market.

Her heartbeat quickened as the tavern came into view. In her right-hand pocket, her fingers closed over the letter knife she had put there on impulse, just in case she needed it to defend herself. Or the rubies.

A coach with two restive horses had stopped opposite the tavern. The coachman seemed to be asleep, his head almost lost in the upturned collar of his coat. As she drew nearer, she saw that the window was covered by black curtains.

A sailor lay on the tavern steps, snoring. As Frances approached, a scantily dressed female stepped over him and went on her way, yawning. Frances took a deep breath.

"Oi!" called a voice from the street.

She glanced over her shoulder, not truly expecting the hail to be aimed at her. But it was the wiry man with the darting eyes who had tried to sell her the ring and the sapphire bracelet, and he was striding toward her.

He stopped and jerked his head toward the stationary coach. Frances walked warily to the man.

"Got something for you," he said casually, glancing up and down the street.

"Really?" she asked eagerly. "What I was looking for?"

He nodded and jerked open the coach door. "In here. Quick."

Every instinct rebelled. "No. Just give me them and tell me what you want."

"It's taken care of, but I'm not stupid enough to hand them over in the public street, am I? Get in. A friend of yours is there already."

"Get in, boy," a husky, foreign voice said from the depths of the coach. "We're all friends here."

Recognizing the voice with relief, Frances climbed up. The wiry man came so close at her heels that she was almost bundled inside and the door slammed shut.

Frances landed on the comfortable seat in almost total darkness. The figure in the corner, her Russian, turned his head from the window, but she could not make out his face.

"You," the Russian said, "are not meant to be here."

She lifted her chin, though she doubted he could see her defiance in the dark. "I didn't choose to let you do it alone."

"Give him the rubies," the Russian ordered.

The wiry man on the opposite bench delved inside his coat. An instant later, the familiar case was thrust into her hands. She all but tore it open on her lap, but could see nothing inside. She ran her fingers over the interior, feeling the cold, shapely stones, the sharper diamonds among the gold setting. She let out a sigh that was almost a sob.

"Thank you," she whispered, trying to force herself to think beyond the sheer relief, Disaster had somehow been averted and she could face Torridon with the truth. She swallowed. "Have we agreed a price?"

"We have," the Russian said. "It is taken care of. He knows he's well rid of them." He reached across the gap and money rustled, changing hands.

Without another word, the wiry man slipped out of the coach, temporarily blinding Frances with a flash of daylight before the door slammed shut again. The Russian knocked on the roof and the carriage began to move immediately. Apparently, the coachman was not as asleep as Frances had thought.

She hugged the rubies to her breast. "I was so afraid I'd never see them again! Thank you from the bottom of my heart, sir! Did that man have them all along, then?"

"No, but he gave them to you, which is the main thing."

"Yes, but—" She broke off, frowning. "Where are we going?"

"To the hotel, where you can change into something more respectable and collect your child. And then to the castle."

"I shall be glad if you drop me at the back of the hotel," she said firmly. "But you need not wait. I shall go to the castle later."

"Sooner would be better," he observed. "You probably don't know that Lord and Lady Tamar depart first thing tomorrow morning. This will be your last chance for months, probably, to spend time with your sister."

"Tomorrow?" she said in dismay. Had she imagined time would stop for her foolish adventures? That everyone would change their plans accordingly?

The coach turned off the high street into the lane leading around to the back of the hotel.

"The carriage will wait for you at the front door," the Russian said and pressed a fat purse into her hands. "To pay your account, if necessary."

She nodded gratefully, having forgotten all about the small matter of the hotel bill in all the excitement of retrieving the rubies. She jumped down without the aid of the steps. There was a certain liberation about being a boy.

Slamming the coach door, she slouched away into the kitchen.

A few minutes later, she slipped back into her own rooms. Jamie

---

had fallen asleep on his blanket with a shawl over him. Lawson sat on the sofa, stuffing piles of clothing into bags.

"All is well," Frances said gaily. "Is Mrs. Marshall awake?"

"Awake and out again, my lady, but she said she wouldn't be long. We're packing up, as you see."

"And I, Lawson."

It was a matter of minutes to change, with Lawson to help lace her up, and to brush and pin her hair before donning the widow's veil one last time. Then she packed the few possessions she'd brought with her—including the rubies—into her portmanteau. She folded up Joe's clothes and asked Lawson to return them to the porter when she had a moment. She had already paid him handsomely for the loan.

"I was hoping Mrs. Marshall would be back by now," Frances said, "but I have to go. Tell her I will be at the castle if she cares to call before she leaves—as herself, not Mrs. Thom! And that either way I shall write to her." She bent and picked up the sleeping baby, wrapping him in another shawl.

The porter who came to carry her portmanteau turned out to be Joe, who grinned at her and promised to return for his old clothes, confiding that he had bought himself a new suit for Sundays. With that, he walked off to bestow her luggage in the waiting coach.

"I've left a small gift for you on my bed," Frances told Lawson, who was wistfully stroking Jamie's cheek. "In appreciation of all you've done."

Jamie opened his eyes and smiled at Lawson who, inevitably, smiled back.

"It was a pleasure," the maid said, far more softly than she usually addressed adults. "But thank you, my lady."

"If I can ever be of assistance to you," Frances said, "please don't hesitate to call on me."

"Thank you, I will."

"Goodbye, Lawson."

"Goodbye, my lady."

Pulling the veil over her face, she left the room and walked downstairs to pay her bill—which was indeed considerably more than she had left without the Russian's contribution. Especially after the reckless gratuity she had left for Lawson. Then Mrs. Alan walked out of the hotel, rewarding the doorman as she went, and stepped into the waiting coach, which, still in darkness, set off at once.

She took off her veil and sat back on the comfortable seat. She was Lady Torridon once more.

"How did you know who I was?" she asked the Russian, who sat in his dark corner, making no attempt to come closer or brush against her. She was grateful. It was going to be hard enough to mix socially with him in the same room as her husband.

"The housekeeper, Mrs. Gaskell, told me the letter you sent was from Lady Frances."

"That was a flaw in my plan," Frances admitted. "I never thought she would give me away."

"I don't imagine she meant to."

"Are you… are you acquainted with my husband?" she asked.

"Yes. I know he loves you to distraction."

Her throat ached suddenly with tears. "Does he?" she whispered wistfully.

The carriage rumbled out of the town, taking the hill up to the castle.

"Do you love him?" the Russian asked.

"Only him. Always him." A choke of laughter mixed with her tears. "For what it's worth, if there had ever been anyone else, it would probably have been you. I owe you so much and I don't even know your name. Or what you look like unmasked!"

"Don't you?"

She frowned, but the coach jolted over a stone at that moment, throwing her forward. The Russian threw out his arm to save her, but by some instinct to preserve her son from harm, she was already holding grimly onto the seat and hauled herself back into safety. Jamie woke up and began to cry.

"Hush, little man," she begged, and rocked him until the crying stopped and his eyes closed once more.

By then, the carriage had turned inside the gates and was almost at the castle.

"I wish I had not stayed at the hotel," she said ruefully. "I wish I had stayed here so we could all have been together for longer."

"There will be other times," he said, although of course, he could not know that.

The carriage pulled up at the front steps and a footman ran out to let down the steps. Bright daylight entered the dark coach, almost blinding her once more. The Russian brushed past her, his face still averted, and alighted before turning at the door to help her.

Concentrating on the steps, she held Jamie in one arm and took the Russian's hand to descend. Only when she stood on the ground did she glance up to thank him.

The world tilted and her stomach dived. For she looked into the face of her husband.

Chapter Ten

A FAINT RUEFUL smile played about his lips. But his eyes were veiled, unreadable, as though he had no idea how she would respond. Neither had Frances.

She knew she stared. She knew she stood perfectly still with her jaw dropped, but those were merely her body's reactions. Inside, she felt stunned, unable to think, or even to believe her own eyes.

"You," she whispered. "It was always you."

His fingers tightened on hers. He leaned nearer, and panic sliced through her numbness. At the same time, a cry went up from the front door and her three youngest sisters spilled down the front steps.

Behind them, Serena cried, *"Frances!"*

With a sound like a sob, Frances spun away from her husband to embrace her sisters all at once and then individually, laughing and crying at the same time. The floodgates of her emotions had opened and her whole being churned with them.

"Oh, and this is Jamie," Serena exclaimed, finally registering the bewildered bundle in Frances's arm. "He is beautiful! Girls, admire your nephew."

The girls duly did, with some awe, as if Frances had been incredibly clever to produce the tiny being.

Although her sisters were dressed for walking, they immediately dragged her into the house, all talking at once, asking questions and imparting vital news. She didn't once look back at Torridon. She couldn't.

"Gervaise!" Helen yelled as soon as she was inside. "Mama!

Frances is home!"

I am. I am home, thank God...

"Helen, you hoyden, you are not a fishwife!" Serena scolded.

Frances laughed. "I remember you doing the same thing when Gervaise came home from school the first time. I heard you from the other side of the castle. But I have a confession to make." There was no point in telling Torridon first. He already knew. He'd known from the moment she had opened her mouth in the draper's shop. Because, unlike him, she hadn't disguised her voice. "I have been in Blackhaven for several days. I even came to the ball, and not one of you knew me!"

"Oh, Fran," Serena said indignantly, as the younger ones swept her upstairs. "Why didn't you say? Why didn't you stay here? I'm leaving *tomorrow!*"

"I know," Frances said guiltily. "Torridon has just told me. I suppose you had been putting it off for so long, I hoped you would never go!"

"Of course I must go," Serena said gruffly. "Just as you went to Scotland."

Frances met her gaze over the girls' heads. "I never meant us to end up at opposite ends of the country."

The girls pulled her into the drawing room, where a young woman stood to greet her. A beautiful woman with red-gold hair who looked at once proud and nervous. They had spoken at the ball.

"Now, I must present you to Gervaise's new countess! Dawn, this is my sister Frances, otherwise Lady Torridon. Frances, this is Eleanor, though we all tend to call her Dawn."

Frances smiled, going forward alone to meet her. "How do you do? I know there is a story behind these names that I only know part of. You must tell me all, if you please!"

They had barely touched hands before a deafening rustle of silks announced the arrival of the dowager countess.

"Mama!" Frances went to her at once, kissing her cool cheek.

Her mother, who rarely betrayed emotion although she felt it keenly enough, gripped her tightly for a moment before releasing her and searching her face. Her eyes narrowed. "You have been up to mischief."

Frances choked on a laugh. "I have and I owe both you and Eleanor a special apology."

"Don't I get one?" Gervaise inquired, strolling into the room.

"No, for you didn't recognize me either!" Frances retorted, hugging him.

"It was you, wasn't it?" Alice blurted. "The lady who sent us inside away from those stupid men?"

"Well, once an oldest sister, one never loses the bossiness," Frances said vaguely, with a quick frown at Alice in passing before the girl betrayed herself further. "Oh, and I danced with your husband, Serena, and I like him excessively."

She knew the instant Torridon entered the room, but she would not look at him. Behind the pleasure of being once more in the center of her family, guilt for what she had done rose up from her toes along with shame at what her husband had witnessed, what she had said to him, asked of him... dear God, she had even let him kiss her, though thank God she had sent him away...

Yet among all of that, indignation simmered into anger. He had been playing with her, manipulating her—which, perhaps, she deserved. But more than that, he had been *testing* her. And that made her feel... *unclean*. Somehow, the shock of him being the Russian made everything worse rather than better, crumbling all her elation in the retrieval of the rubies, and eating away at the pleasure of her family reunion.

"It's almost time for luncheon," Serena said at last. "Shall we postpone our walk until after that? Oh, and we shall have guests for dinner tonight."

"You still have guests who came north for the ball?" Frances asked.

"Oh, no, they have all left already. Apart from Sylvester, Tamar's brother, who is travelling south with us tomorrow. No, these are local people, particular friends of mine and Tamar's—a farewell dinner."

"But you won't be gone forever, Serena," Helen said anxiously.

"Of course, I won't," Serena agreed. "And when you go to London with Mama, I'm sure she'll bring you to stay at Tamar Abbey, too. Come on, Frances, I'll help you with your things before luncheon. I have so much to tell you."

Frances, anxious to avoid a tête-à-tête with her husband until everything stopped churning inside her, leapt at the chance of Serena's company. He still stood by the door, as if refusing to be part of her welcoming family.

He raised his arms. "Let me take Jamie for now."

"Oh no, he will want to be fed again soon, and I want to show him off to Serena."

Torridon made no objection, merely let his arms fall and strolled further into the room.

Frances felt the urge to have her old bedchamber, but Serena began walking at once toward Torridon's, which had been redecorated for both of them on their marriage. To avoid fuss, Frances complied. Besides, everything was such a muddle, she had no idea how she felt about sharing his rooms, let alone his bed.

Frances laid Jamie in the center of the huge bed and she and Serena sat on either side of him. Serena tickled his cheeks to make him smile and talked nonsense to him for a little. Then she lifted her gaze to Frances. "I am expecting a child, too," she blurted.

Frances smiled. "I thought there was something. Is that what you've been trying not to say in your last letters?"

"I wanted to tell you in person. There was even some scheme to come and see you, but somehow it never happened."

"I am so pleased for you," Frances whispered, as tears started to her eyes. "And Tamar is so *right* for you."

"As Torridon is for you?"

Frances looked away. "Of course."

Serena stroked Jamie's soft hair while her perceptive gaze remained on Frances. "Have you quarreled?"

"How did you guess?"

"Intuition," Serena said with a half-smile. "And the fact that he has clearly been worried sick waiting for you while you have been in Blackhaven all this time making no effort to see any of us."

"He knew where I was," Frances said in a hard, little voice. "He always knew. He simply chose not to tell me or you. But let's not talk of that nonsense. Tell me how you've been?"

"Apart from a little sick in the mornings, I'm very well. Dr. Lampton is pleased with me, at any rate."

They talked of pregnancy, Tamar Abbey, and the friends who were coming to dinner that evening.

"Gillie and Wickenden will be there, of course. And the Grants and the Benedicts. The famous Captain Alban and Lady Arabella—who is also increasing!—and Lord and Lady Daxton."

"Daxton?" Frances said, startled, as she lifted Jamie to her breast for feeding. "Is that a good idea, Serena?"

"You mean that nonsense last autumn?" Serena said disparagingly. "It was a storm in a teacup. Though to be frank, I am very glad of it, for if my engagement had not been broken over it, I would never have been able to marry Tamar and then I would have been miserable. Besides, Dax is an old friend of Tamar's. They were at school together. You'll like Lady Dax, too."

"Hmm, tell me about Eleanor, whom you all call Dawn."

"Ah, now that you must hear!"

As Serena told her the amazing story of how Gervaise had met and married his countess, Frances listened, rapt, until the door opened quietly and Torridon came in.

Serena broke off at once.

"Ignore me," Torridon said mildly. "I only came to change my boots."

"No, no," Serena said, jumping up. Frances had to prevent herself seizing her sister's arm to make her stay. "I was going anyway. We have gossiped long enough, and we can talk more over luncheon."

Torridon courteously held the door for Serena, who fled with a vague smile. For the first time, it struck Frances that Serena was not on the same easy terms with Torridon as she was with most people. Torridon, of course, was a difficult combination of reserved and intimidating. It was his sheer presence that had first drawn Frances to him. Amongst the light-weight fashionable fribbles of London society, he had risen up before her like a Colossus. A serious man with laughing eyes. A man of sense as well as wit. Her protector, her lover. Or so she had thought...

He closed the door behind Serena and walked to the bed, his eyes on his feeding son. For the first time, she felt exposed in this position. Blood seeped into her face.

He stroked his son's head, which disturbed Jamie not at all. It was a familiar touch.

Torridon said, "You are shocked."

"You meant me to be."

His lips twisted. "I hoped it would be a pleasant surprise."

She raised her indignant gaze to his face.

He sighed and perched on the bed facing her and Jamie. "We should talk, Frances. You wanted to talk to me, remember?"

"There is no point now," she retorted. "You already know every-thing."

"I know what you chose to tell a stranger," he said steadily. "Start at the beginning. Why did you bolt from Torridon without a word?"

"Because if I had spoken that word, you and your servants and your mother and her servants would all have conspired to stop me."

A frown twitched his brow. "But what was behind it? Why did you wish to go so badly?"

Because I could not bear to be trapped a minute longer. Because I need to live. Because you never cared for me. Because I won't be just another part of your estate. She swallowed the words back, pride refusing to let her admit her hurt.

"Were you so unhappy?" he asked.

She would not look at him, merely nodded. She wished he would shout at her, scold her, argue so that she could shout back. She wanted to hit him.

And yet, the tension in his shoulders told her this was difficult for him. He was not a man who easily discussed his feelings. He took a breath. "I am not so silly as to believe that one quarrel made you so. But you told *him*, my alter ego, that you loved me."

She stared fixedly at Jamie's blurred head, daring the tears to fall.

"Is there nothing you want to ask me?" he asked softly.

Do you love me? Did you ever love me? The words stuck in her throat.

"Yes," she drawled. "Would you please ring for a maid to watch Jamie? And we'll need a cradle for him."

Laying the sleeping baby in the center of the bed, she covered him with a shawl with one hand, while she covered herself with the other.

After a moment, Torridon rose and pulled the bell. She took the opportunity to try and slip past him, but at the last moment, he caught her wrist and spun her back against him.

God, she remembered his body, all heat and hardness. How had she not known the Russian was him? Had it really been so long? She should have recognized his expressive, dark eyes, the sensual mouth which had kissed her so intimately. Or perhaps some part of her had known. Why else would she have trusted him so quickly? Why else would she have been so attracted, so tempted?

"Don't shut me out, Frances," he whispered. "We have a chance to make this better, to make it right. Talk to me."

She stared at him, her throat aching once more. "You deliberately manipulated me, provoked me, *tested* me," she burst out. "How do I forgive that?"

Something flashed in his eyes, something that changed and resolved into neither anger nor shame, but the predatory stare of the hunter. Her breath caught. There was only his muscular body against her, his fingers on her galloping pulse, his parted lips only inches from her own, and the flare of sweet, hot desire.

And then a knock at the door made her whisk herself free as a maid came in. "Ah, Kitty, it's you," she babbled, recognizing the girl who had been with her family for years. "This is Jamie, our son. Will you sit with him until the others bring down a cradle for him? Thank you."

Even as she hurried along the passage, she knew she was fleeing her husband again, though this time for different reasons. Suddenly, he seemed so much more than she'd ever imagined, a man of layers and complexities, an elusive man so far beyond her reach that it was frightening.

TORRIDON KNEW HE had shaken her, and while her reaction was not what he had expected, he hung onto two things that gave him hope. She had told "the Russian" she loved her husband, with a genuineness he couldn't doubt. And when he caught her in the bedchamber, though she bridled like a skittish colt, her pulse galloped under his fingers. Her quickened breath did not come from fear. She was not immune to the desire that flared between them. He needed patience, as he always had with Frances.

And so, he did not take the place next to her at luncheon, but sat by Serena instead in order to give his wife space to get used to his presence once more. Since the children were present—unusual in a great family—there was a good deal of chatter and laughter. The dowager countess was disposed to be tolerant and seemed much more human among them.

Torridon found himself thinking of his own mother, whom he'd seen very little of, growing up. In fact, she had never been around so much as in the last year, after he had married Frances. *Protecting her own position*, he thought unkindly. And immediately felt uncomfortable, not because the thought was unfilial, but because it had the ring of truth.

For the first time, Torridon began to question his reliance on his mother for advice during Frances's pregnancy and her lying-in. And after. Frances had been galivanting around the country, caring for the child without an army of servants, and both she and Jamie appeared to be thriving.

He shoved the thought aside for later, and instead, let himself be drawn into several conversations at once—with Braithwaite and Tamar on the newest land improvement schemes, with the girls about visiting Scotland, and the current loyalty of the Scots to the king, and with Eleanor, the young countess whom he rather liked, on her fascinating life before she had come to Blackhaven.

"You have settled in as though you have always been here," he observed under cover of other chatter, for it struck him that Eleanor's position as a young wife with a domineering mother-in-law was quite similar to Frances's. "You have no... disagreements with the dowager."

Eleanor laughed. "Oh, we have many. But we have reached an understanding. The armed truce between us is now close to friendship."

Across the table, Frances was listening to Serena's over-excited chatter about her new home at Tamar Abbey. His wife's face was focused and thoughtful, and her sheer beauty made his heart turn over.

He dragged his gaze back to Eleanor. "And how did you reach this understanding?"

Eleanor lowered her voice. "I asked her for help when I needed it. I still do, and from the understanding I learn from her, I am finding my own way."

Torridon glanced from the young countess to the old. A new respect for his mother-in-law formed alongside the knowledge that his own mother was incapable of such flexibility. There was only her way or the wrong way.

Serena seemed to have calmed a little under Frances's influence, losing much of the hectic anxiety that had characterized her during Torridon's stay. Frances laughed at something Sylvester Gaunt said, quickly drawing Serena into the joke.

Torridon's heart twisted. The sisters had missed each other. And that they had been so much apart was largely his fault. Frances glanced up and met his gaze. She turned away almost immediately, a hint of color seeping into her face.

After lunch, everyone who was choosing to go, prepared for their walk.

"I'll bring Jamie," Frances said, and then glanced at Torridon with defiance. Which surprised him until he remembered his mother's views of exposing infants to the damp and cold of outdoors. "Just let me dash off a quick letter and I'll fetch him."

"I'll fetch him while you write," Torridon said and went upstairs to relieve Kitty the maid, who wrapped Jamie in two shawls, much to Jamie's annoyance, before passing him to his father.

Jamie stopped crying and gave him a toothless grin.

"I should think so, young man," Torridon observed. "Now, one for Kitty, if you please, to apologize for your ill manners."

Kitty laughed, tickling the baby's cheek, and Jamie grinned at her, too. Torridon bore him off, with his great coat over his free arm. He found his wife alone in the smaller of the downstairs reception rooms, seated at the spindly desk where she was folding a letter.

Again, there was a hint of defiance in her expression as she glanced up. "I am writing to Mrs. Marshall since I did not see her when I left."

"Very proper," he replied. "Where is everyone else?"

"Oh, they will all gather eventually. Or follow. Organizing any expedition from this house is like herding cats. Ah, John," she added, as a footman appeared at the door. "Would you have this delivered to the hotel?"

"Of course, my lady. A Mrs. Marshall has called for you."

"Oh!" Halfway across the room, she halted in surprise. "Well, never mind the letter then. Show her in, John." As John turned to do her bidding, she glanced at Torridon. "Give me the baby, if you wish."

"Oh, no," Torridon said, "We are quite comfortable."

He bowed as Mrs. Marshall rushed in crying, "Oh, Frannie, thank goodness! Listen, I have been thinking and—" Mrs. Marshall broke off, apparently flabbergasted by the sight of him. She'd always known he was here, so he could only suppose she hadn't been expecting him to inhabit the same room as his wife.

"My lord," she greeted him coolly enough with a slightly ironic curtsey.

"Madam." He sat down with Jamie and dangled his pocket watch above the baby's head. Jamie made a grab for it with his fat little hands and dragged it toward his mouth. Torridon drew is back.

"I'm so glad you came," Frances said warmly. "I have just been writing to you. Are you going to stay in Blackhaven?"

"Lord, no, I'm on my way south as we speak, only I have been thinking about your wretched ... problem and ... why don't we take a walk?"

"Oh, don't mind your tongue in front of Torridon," Frances said. "He knows everything."

Mrs. Marshall blinked. "He does? Then he probably agrees with me that we should involve the authorities after all. I think I know who took them and it is just silly to—"

"But we don't need to worry any more, Ari," Frances interrupted. "That's what I've been writing to tell you. We have the rubies back. Torridon got them."

Mrs. Marshall's gaze flew to his face. "Did he?" If the news shook her, she hid it very well.

"But who do you think took them?" Frances demanded, drawing her friend onto the other sofa beside her.

Mrs. Marshall sighed, firing a warning look toward Torridon. "I very much fear it was the supposed gentleman who called on me. I confess I left him alone for a few minutes while you were out. To be honest, I really don't see how anyone else could have got into our rooms, so though it pains me, Frannie, it must be him. What you do about it is your own affair, of course, but there, I have said my piece and must go." She rose to her feet once more. "Goodbye, Frances. Write to me and no doubt I'll see you in London one day."

"Frances!" came Lady Maria's voice from the stairs.

Frances rose and embraced her friend. "Goodbye, Ariadne, and thank you for everything! Let me see you to your carriage."

"Frances!" Lady Alice added her voice to the growing cacophony.

Torridon stood. "You had better resolve your sisters' crises," he advised, "and I shall walk with Mrs. Marshall in your stead."

With a quick, distracted smile, Frances hurried from the room. Torridon followed more slowly and politely held the door for Mrs. Marshall.

"Is this where you lecture me?" she drawled, walking past him, "for leading your wife astray?"

"No. This is where I tell you that you may continue to correspond with my wife as you and she choose, but that you will have no closer contact with her."

That surprised her. Well, he probably didn't look terribly threatening strolling across the huge entrance hall with a baby in his arms. But her stunned look quickly faded into a tinkling laugh.

"My dear Torridon, whatever control you have—or imagine you should have—over your wife, you have absolutely none over me."

"On the contrary. You see, I know exactly who stole the rubies from my wife."

"What a busy person you must be. Then you know whom I meant when I mentioned the gentleman—"

"Sylvester Gaunt did not steal my wife's rubies," he interrupted, tired of her games. "You did."

Her skin might have paled slightly, but she still managed a derisive laugh. "Oh, please. I know you don't like me, but I am not the devil incarnate!"

"Of course you are not. You are merely an unprincipled woman who is short of money. You staked your paste 'diamonds' against my wife's rubies in the hope of winning your wager. And when you saw me in Blackhaven, you were sure of winning. But just in case you didn't, you set up poor Gaunt to take the blame if necessary for the theft, which was your alternative plan."

"It is a pleasant fantasy, my lord," she sneered.

"Not for me. You took the rubies when no one appeared to know Frances at the ball. The irony is, you had won, because I knew her all along."

Ariadne actually laughed, an odd, slightly bitter sound, but there was genuine amusement in there, too. "Without proof, my lord, it is still fantasy."

"I have proof, madam," he said grimly. "It was I who took the diamonds from your room, from the bedside cabinet while you dined with my wife, and your maid looked after my son."

Her feet faltered for the first time and she stared at him. Mockery and genuine fear battled in her eyes.

He stopped with her, just in front of the great carved front door. "That's what sent you up here, isn't it? You were, no doubt, packing to leave when you discovered the rubies really had been stolen. Now, you actually *do* want the thief caught, hence your recommendation to finally involve the authorities. But in case of difficulty, poor Gaunt was to remain a suspect."

She turned away, but her fingers trembled as she fumbled with the door.

Torridon opened it for her. "I will not have you repeat such slander. The lad has had a difficult enough life."

She waved that aside as unimportant and walked out of the door. He followed and they stood a moment on the front step.

"You haven't told Frances," she said, and lifted her eyes to his. "Will you?"

He shook his head. "No. She is unhappy enough without the hurt of your false friendship."

"Oh, the friendship was real enough," she said ruefully. "But one must live." She descended one step.

"If you don't comply with my conditions," he said coldly, "I will be compelled to tell her. Don't force me to do that."

She laughed. "My dear Torridon, I have never been able to force or even persuade you into anything." She turned back to him consideringly. "How strange. I believe you actually do love her."

Then she sailed down the rest of the steps and climbed into the waiting chaise. Torridon took his son back inside.

Chapter Eleven

ARIADNE GOT AS far as the next coastal town of Whalen before rage overtook her utterly.

She had never taken well to being told what to do, particularly when it contradicted what she wished to do. And that *he* of all people should compel her to leave his wife alone, as if Ariadne Marshall were some vulgar lover instead of the only friend who indulged Frances's love of mischief…

In any case, that was simply the last straw, the insult added to the injury of defeating her. How dared he enter her rooms and simply take the rubies? She could not even have him punished for it, since the rooms were his wife's and the rubies his. Damn him, they must have been in his pocket when he approached her and Frances at dinner that night!

Wretched man. Are you on this earth merely to thwart and torment me?

And to think she had once come close to loving him. She had thought him elusive, suspected him of using her own tactics of not appearing to care in order to encourage notice, interest, obsession. But she had been wrong. He really hadn't noticed her and he had had no interest in her whatsoever. It was Frances who had claimed all his attention.

And still did. He was protecting Frances from her and from any hurt she might feel if she learned the truth, that her friend had stolen from her, had let her suffer all that anxiety over losing the rubies. She had even let Frances dress as a boy and walk alone into the sailors' tavern. Actually, Ariadne would have liked to be there for that adventure.

But still, she had been punished. The moment she had discovered the rubies were gone from her bedside cabinet had been equal, surely, to Frances's horror. She had yelled at Lawson and only just stopped short of accusing the hotel staff. She couldn't accuse anyone when she shouldn't have had them anyway.

Torridon had had her defeated and sewn up, and now she was dismissed like a servant who tippled at her master's port. By him. He always had to find some new way to get under her skin.

"Damn him," she whispered.

"I beg your pardon, ma'am?" Lawson inquired.

Ariadne ignored her. *There is a way. There has to be a way. I will not lose. And God help me, I need the money.*

She had an appointment. But one day would surely not matter… especially if she was successful. Her breath caught. She stared at Lawson, then abruptly knocked on the roof to make the driver stop. "Tell them to take us to the most respectable inn in the town and pay them off."

AFTER THEIR WALK, Frances followed Maria to her new bedchamber.

"This used to be Grandmama's chamber," Frances recalled.

"Gervaise and Dawn said I could pick whichever I wanted," Maria said defensively. "As you and Serena both did."

"Of course. It wasn't a criticism. I like the room much better now. It's lighter and brighter—like you!" Frances sat on the bed, admiring the hangings and the ornaments. "I can't believe you are sixteen already. You must be looking forward to your London season next year."

Maria fiddled a little nervously with the curtain. "Of course."

"I suppose Eleanor will be able to present you at court by then. And I shall make sure I am there to dance at your coming-out ball. Serena must come, too."

"Oh, don't, Frances." Maria swung on her, much too agitated for the conversation. "Why must I always do what you and Serena did? Why is it all laid out for me?"

"I suppose it's what ladies of our class do. We have a little fun while attracting the most suitable husband. Like it or not, that is the most comfortable life for us and our families. Beyond that, your life will be what you make it."

Of course, Frances herself hadn't done such a terribly good job of that, so far, but she had at least produced Jamie. However, that did not make her a shining example for her confused little sister.

"Don't you like the idea anymore?" she asked Maria. "You used to."

"I was a silly little girl," Maria whispered.

"So, what do you want now?" Frances pursued.

Maria shook her head. "I don't know. I never expected it to be this complicated."

Frances stood and went to stand beside her at the window. "Is the complication anything to do with the handsome young officer I saw you with in Blackhaven?"

Maria's gaze flew to her face. "You saw us?"

Frances nodded.

"Then you recognized him among the men on the terrace at the ball?"

Frances nodded again.

"I thought he was perfect," Maria whispered. "Brave and handsome and deeply in love with me."

"Even the best have feet of clay. Why does he not call on us at the castle? Why the secret assignations?"

"Because they're—" Maria began impetuously, and broke off.

"More fun?" Frances guessed.

Maria looked away.

"I can't choose who you care for," Frances said. "No one can. But for what it's worth, if I were you, I would think less of a man who got in quite such a state in my family home. I would think even less of a man who would not brave my brother or even my mother for me."

Maria closed her eyes. Frances guessed she had been trying very hard not to think less of him for these reasons recently, and not entirely succeeding.

Frances took her sister's hand. "You're bored, aren't you?"

Maria nodded. "I don't want to be in the schoolroom anymore. I'm not a child. Gideon never looked on me as a child. And yet, I have to wait a whole year to do *anything*!"

"No, you don't. There are lots of things you can do in London before you come out! And besides that, I would love you to stay with us in Scotland. Maybe just you for a little, while the others brave the new governess Mama has lined up in London."

Maria's eyes brightened, then faded. "Maybe," she said uncertainly.

Frances raised her brows in obvious surprise. "You would rather just stay here? For him? If I were you, I would make him work a little harder for your forgiveness."

"Maybe he has suffered enough," Maria muttered. "Someone hit him at the ball, you know, bruised his cheek."

"Yes, that was Torridon."

Maria blanched. "*Torridon?* But why?"

"Because he, or the company he kept, insulted you, your little sisters, and me."

Maria leaned her back against the wall, then slid down it until she sat on the floor with her knees under her chin, exactly like the child she did not wish to be.

"You think Gideon should have done that," she said in a small, hard voice. "Stopped them insulting us. Don't you?"

"I don't think he was in any state to deal with his friends *or* points of honor. To be frank, Maria, I don't like to think of you alone with him at all."

"Oh, but he is not like that as a rule," Maria assured her. "It was the wine and he has promised me he has given it up."

"Well, I would make him prove it. While I enjoyed the fun of a London season."

Maria regarded her unhappily. "But what if you had met Torridon when you were sixteen? Would you have been so much in favor of waiting then?"

"Good question." Considering it, Frances knelt beside her sister. "I don't know that I would. But when I was sixteen, Torridon was already a seasoned officer in Wellington's army. I expect he was wild and reckless. But I know he would never have behaved other than as a gentleman. And whatever the excitement of his presence, I would always have felt pleasurably safe. No one would have dared insult me or my little sisters."

She began the speech to make her sister think, to show her how she would be throwing herself away on someone like this lightweight Gideon. But she found she was speaking the truth with a wistful, almost dreamy air. Every word was true. There had never been a thrill like meeting Alan, loving Alan...

Realizing Maria was staring at her, she pulled herself back together. "We all make mistakes—Serena and I made lots! I think it's how we learn. But I would really hate for you to make the kind of mistake that you couldn't ever recover from, one that could only lead to unhappiness. If Gideon loves you as you deserve, he will always be there, and he will be glad to meet your family." *Not disgrace you.* With difficulty, she swallowed the last back, wise enough to realize that she would make more of an impression on Maria if she didn't feel compelled to defend her so-called love.

Frances rose to her feet.

"Have you told Mama?" Maria blurted.

"No. And I won't unless I think you're in danger. Don't put yourself in danger, Maria. Men can hurt more than your feelings."

Maria jumped up and hugged her fiercely. "I'm glad you're back," she said and released her.

Frances was touched, but as she left to go to her own chamber, she knew Maria was only half-convinced. Part of her was still set on self-destruction, through boredom or unhappiness or both. Frances knew she would have to watch her carefully. It was as well she had come home.

LORD AND LADY Wickenden arrived at the castle late in the afternoon, bringing with them both their baby and their nursemaid. Gillie, whom Frances had known all her life, glowed with health and happiness, and Wickenden, although he kept his sardonic humor, seemed to have lost that edge of unhappiness that had made him slightly dangerous. Not that he had ever shown Frances anything other than careless kindness, even extracting her from the odd scrape she had got herself into during her first season. But now he made no effort to hide his pride in his tiny son, and Frances felt rather pleased that she had played her part in bringing him and Gillie together last year.

"How much everything has changed in one year," Serena said as she stood with Frances and Gillie, gazing down upon the babies. "If you were even expecting little Jamie then, no one knew it. I was engaged to someone else entirely, and no one thought you, Gillie, would catch the biggest prize on the marriage mart. And now, here we are, all married with children!" Serena placed her hand over her still perfectly flat stomach. "Or at least in a happy condition."

"So much has happened," Frances agreed. And yet most of it had passed her by. She had a son, the most monumental event in her life. But it almost seemed that the rest of her life had stopped. Until this last couple of weeks.

"I wish we had time for Tamar to paint us all together," Serena said ruefully. "And then I could have taken the picture with me to remind me."

"Serena, you're not going to another country," Frances said. "You will be visited—more than you like, I dare say! And you will come back. It's your condition affecting your mood. You know you are not really sad to be going to Tamar's home. You will be in your element, arranging things just as you want them. You have no interfering mother-in-law and you already know his siblings, don't you?"

She wished immediately that she hadn't blurted out the mother-in-law part, but Serena didn't appear to notice, perhaps taking it as a reference to their own mother and Eleanor.

"Yes, I know most of them," Serena admitted. "Apart from Julian, who is Rupert's heir until I produce a son! Sylvester is fun, though shockingly dissipated for one so young. I shall take him in hand. Christianne is sweet and kind and lives in London. And Anna… well, I liked Anna, but she is in Europe, and I suspect secretly helping Britain's interests in the coming peace."

"They are an interesting family," Gillie exclaimed. "You will thrive among them, Serena. We all have our own lives now, but we are not so far apart either."

"I know." Serena smiled. "Blackhaven has become like the center of the universe. All the people who are to dine with us tonight met here and married here, for the most part, and all in the last year. They all have their own lives, too, and yet here they are back in Blackhaven. If they ever left!"

Frances didn't really know the other guests, apart from Kate Grant and Dax, a little. And Mrs. Benedict, she reminded herself, who had once been Miss Grey, her little sisters' governess. But she wasn't sure she wished to be subjected to an evening of deliriously happy married couples. It would, surely, only draw attention to the unhappiness of her own marriage.

However, since she could not change things, she resolved simply to enjoy the company, and went to change for dinner.

When she opened the bedchamber door, she was stupidly stunned to find her husband there, bare-chested, reaching for the clean shirt on the bed.

Her stomach dived and she almost closed the door again, but her entry had been too impetuous, and he had already seen her. She would not run away. She sailed into the room as though the sight of his semi-naked torso meant nothing to her.

"You look surprised to see me," he said, unhurriedly pulling his shirt over his head.

"I suppose I am. It has been a long time since we shared a bed-chamber."

"I am looking forward to sharing this one."

With his shirt hanging loose, and his hair tousled, he looked gloriously rumpled, almost as he had used to look after making love to her. The memory caused her whole body to flush, which annoyed her excessively.

"Why?" she snapped, stalking to the wardrobe. "What has changed in the few days since I left Torridon?"

"Nothing." His eyes were wary and yet avid as they followed her movements. "Do you imagine I did not want to share your bed?"

She paused, her blue evening gown over her arm, and stared at him. "Was there a guard on my door? Was someone placed mysteriously over you as the earl and master of Torridon? No. So, yes, that is exactly what I imagine."

He walked toward her, a deep frown tugging down his brow. "I am not so brutal that I would endanger you or the baby with my demands. Nor would I inflict myself upon you while you recover from the birth."

She gave a skeptical laugh, shaken by his nearness as he halted in front of her, and determined not to betray the fact. "Why, how noble of you, my lord. But I do not need your excuses any more than I need your attentions. I have given you an heir. And now you have my permission," she added, pointing, "to sleep in the dressing room."

"Jamie's cradle is in there," he said, taking the dress from her shocked arms, "and I have no intention of joining him."

"Ring for the maid, if you please," she said breathlessly.

"I don't please." Deliberately, he threw the dress toward the bed where it landed in a heap of silk.

She stepped back in panic, but he followed, and his arms went around her. An instant later, she felt his fingers unlacing her gown. "What are you doing?"

"Undressing you. I have a notion to be your maid for the evening." He turned her, gently, to make his job easier. She stood rigid, trying not to feel the thrill of his fingers brushing her back. "I believed that if I loved you while you carried our child, I could harm you both."

"I find it hard to imagine a man of your experience would believe such arrant rubbish."

"I do not discuss such intimacies with my married friends," he said dryly.

She twisted her head around to stare up at him. "Then with whom?"

For a moment he was silent. "It was my mother's advice," he said reluctantly. "She also told me I should leave you alone for at least six months after the birth."

"Did she also tell you not to discuss the matter with your wife?"

For the first time that she could remember, color seeped into his cheeks. "No. That was my decision. I knew you would never deny me your bed."

The day dress fell around her feet. In her stays and stockings, she faced away from him once more. It seemed easier that way. "And you imagined I would be happier if you took your pleasure elsewhere?"

His big, tender hands closed over her shoulders, drawing her back against him. "I take pleasure in no one else. I never did, since meeting you, and I never will."

She closed her eyes, longing to believe him. But she no longer knew him. She had never known him. Besides, his words were ambiguous. He could have tumbled any number of women in the last year without any great or true pleasure, just to relieve the itch of unspecific lust.

His lips brushed the sensitive skin joining her neck and shoulder, and her breath shuddered in pleasure. But she forced herself to remain rigid in his hold.

He stepped back, drawing her by the hand to the bed. "Am I to understand that you would have welcomed my... presence?"

"Of course," she managed. "As you said yourself, I would never deny you my bed."

"Except tonight, apparently." He dropped the pale underdress over her head and she thrust her arms through it. He began to fasten the laces. "Would you rather I were the Russian?"

"You *are* the Russian," she said indignantly.

He reached for the blue gown. "And you were 'Mrs. Alan.' We were both pretending. Is there really such a difference?"

"You were *testing* me!"

He turned her to face the looking glass and drew the pins from her hair. "No. I was trying to give you the fun I so foolishly denied you over the last year."

Their eyes met in the glass. She could not breathe.

And then a knock at the door made her jump. She had the feeling Torridon was about to tell whoever it was to go to the devil. He had that look in his eyes as he opened his mouth, and it thrilled her.

"Come in," she called perversely, and Kitty the maid stuck her head around the door.

"Lady Braithwaite sent me, my lady, since your own maid isn't with you."

Torridon stepped back. "You may dress her ladyship's hair. That is beyond my skills."

Tucking his shirt into his pantaloons, he picked a snowy white cravat from the back of a chair and walked away to the smaller mirror.

Chapter Twelve

THE BEDCHAMBER ENCOUNTER with his wife gave Torridon plenty to think about that evening. For the first time, he began seriously to doubt both his mother's agenda and his own reliance upon her opinion. Frances had been so precious to him, and he was so conscious of the fact that his eldest sister had died in childbirth, that he had taken his mother's advice as gospel—which he never had before, not since he was ten years old. He should have discussed such matters with the doctor instead.

Had he really been so blind that he had not seen how his excessive care hurt Frances in so many other ways? Certainly, there had been a shade of grimness about it, caused by his self-imposed celibacy. And perhaps he'd been influenced after all by the austere Presbyterian attitude of so many of his countrymen, that suffering was good for his soul.

Without meaning to, he had put spiritual as well as physical distance between them, all because he wanted to keep her and the baby safe. And he had let his mother rule his wife's house.

"What in God's name was I thinking?"

Since he spoke aloud while walking downstairs with his wife on his arm, she glanced at him askance.

"I have no idea," she replied.

"Are you afraid of me, Frances?"

She blinked. "No. Though you can be intimidating, you were never so with me."

"Then why do you never tell me I'm talking rubbish or that I am just plain wrong? Politeness?"

A frown flickered on her brow. Her eyes were wary. "It depends which particular rubbish you mean."

"About your safety before and after Jamie was born."

Her breath caught and she looked away. "I told you. I took it to be your excuse. *Your* politeness, if you will."

To his annoyance, they had reached the bottom of the stairs and were about to meet up with Serena and Tamar who were approaching the drawing room from the other direction. "You thought I was politely tired of you?" he said urgently.

"Aren't you?" Frances dropped his arm and went at once to Serena.

The adult family members had gathered in the drawing room, along with the Wickendens and Tamar's brother, Lord Sylvester. The next guests to arrive were the famous Captain Alban and his wife Lady Arabella, the Duke of Kelburn's daughter. They were introduced as Mr. and Mrs. Lamont, since apparently, he was related to one of the local landowners.

Torridon, who had vaguely expected a loud, swaggering sailor, was surprised to discover a quietly spoken, serious man. On his arm was a pretty but slightly eccentric looking lady in spectacles. She seemed shy, although Frances soon began to draw her out.

"You're not driving all the way back to Roseley tonight, are you?" Braithwaite said to Alban.

"No, I have a ship anchored close to the harbor. We'll row out there—we sail in the morning anyway."

"Are you comfortable with that?" Serena asked Lady Arabella.

"Oh yes. I hardly ever feel sick, now, and I like being at sea."

Only then did Torridon notice the slight bump beneath Lady Arabella's dress. She was with child. And her husband took her to sea. However, she looked perfectly healthy with such treatment. While Frances, he remembered, had grown pale and listless and increasingly discontented. She hadn't been ill. She had been bored.

His speculations were interrupted by the arrival of the Grants and the Daxtons, both of whom he had met before. In fact, he had known Grant in his army days and was still somewhat stunned to find the man the vicar of St. Andrews in Blackhaven. Remembering him, Torridon didn't share his wife's wonder that he had tamed the wild Kate Crowmore, the wicked lady herself. Well, not tamed. But he'd married her and she was clearly perfectly happy with her life.

Daxton was younger, a contemporary of his friend Tamar. A restless, volatile but rather charming man, he could also talk about serious issues, especially land improvement, about which he knew a surprising amount. His wife was a calmer young lady with laughing eyes and a sweet temperament, already, clearly, a friend of Kate's and Lady Wickenden's.

The final guests to arrive were Colonel and Mrs. Benedict. Torridon had met them at the ball, although in fact he had previously known Mrs. Benedict as Miss Grey, the Braithwaite children's governess. But Benedict was also known to him by reputation: for years he had led an elite troop of fighting men on special tasks behind enemy lines, tasks for which the term "forlorn hope" was never even invoked. A stern man, he also turned out to be humorous and extremely well read for a fighting man. He had even published a new book on botany. And although it was considered an unequal match by some, he and "Miss Grey" seemed perfect for each other.

It was a jolly company. Even the dowager Lady Braithwaite relaxed into benevolence. And Eleanor was a perfect hostess, leading the guests into dinner on Lord Daxton's arm. The conversation was lively and informal, full of wit and laughter, the sort Torridon enjoyed and was not above joining in. Indeed, he cast the odd word here and there, but too frequently, he found his attention wandering back to his wife.

Frances shone. Beautiful, quick-witted, and lively, she charmed the whole company. Torridon found it hard to drag his gaze away from her brilliance. If she was aware of his observation, she gave no sign, although once as he laughed at one of Lady Arabella's unexpectedly droll remarks, he happened to glance up and meet Frances's gaze. Spontaneously, his smile widened, and a response quirked her lips as if she couldn't help it. And then she turned hastily back to her own conversation.

It was a little like falling in love all over again, wondering if the lovely, spirited girl with all the admirers and suitors would even notice him. And his heart would pound at one glance from her. It still did. And he was still trying to win her.

Well, perhaps not "still". That had been the problem. He had stopped trying and risked losing, not his wife, perhaps, but his wife's love.

WHEN THE DINNER guests had departed, Braithwaite proposed a toast to Serena and Tamar, and after that, everyone drifted away, leaving Frances alone with her sister, still talking. Frances knelt on the Persian rug before the fire, while Serena sat in the closest arm chair.

"I should go and feed my child," Frances said at last. "He will be screaming at poor Torridon."

"Poor Torridon," Serena quoted, "yet you say it with considerable satisfaction."

Frances laughed. "Perhaps I do."

Serena leaned forward. "Frances, is everything well between you?"

Frances opened her mouth to lie. But this was Serena. She would know. She already knew. "Not really, no."

"Because of your prank with Ariadne Marshall?"

"Well, that didn't help. I… I am so *crushed*, Serena."

Serena slid down onto the rug beside her. "Oh, my dear, how? Why?"

Frances shook her head. "He looks after me as if I'm porcelain, not flesh and blood. I am all but confined to the house while old Lady Torridon manages the duties I am apparently too weak to cope with. I see no one except her and the minister's wife. And Torridon only at mealtimes if he happens to be in the house."

Serena's eyes widened in shock. "But how has Torridon let this happen? How have you?"

Frances sighed. "I don't know. I suppose I felt precious being coddled, just at first. And then I didn't want to displease him by making a fuss or quarreling with his mother. It happened so slowly, so gradually... and I have been very involved with Jamie, of course..." Frances drew in her breath. "I think... he no longer loves me. Or that he never did. I merely misunderstood a respectable, civilized marriage of convenience. And I cannot bear that he was merely being polite."

"*Torridon?*" Serena said in a startled voice. "Frances, the man is infamous for saying exactly what he thinks. He is brutally honest. I cannot think for one moment that he would declare his love for you if it were not true."

"Well, that's the thing," Frances murmured, gazing into the fire rather than her sister's face. "He never did. I *assumed*. Because I loved *him*, and because he was so very... tender." So much so that there had been times when she had longed for him to lose control, to sweep them both into the wilder passion that she was sure lurked in him... just not for her.

"But... but he is devoted to you," Serena said, sounding bewildered. "It's in his eyes, his face, his every gesture, every time he looks at you. Anyone can see that."

"Can they?" she whispered wistfully.

"He followed you here, didn't he?"

Frances shrugged impatiently. "That was different. He was reclaiming what was his, *testing* what was his to see if I would betray him."

"But you wouldn't!" Serena exclaimed, and then glanced at her askance. "Would you?"

"Oh, for goodness sake, what do you take me for?" Frances demanded.

"I take you to be unhappy. You can do anything when you're unhappy."

"Well, I bolted down here incognito just to win a wager I could not pay if I lost. And so, made things worse."

Serena contemplated that for a little. "What will you do now?"

"I don't know. I'm so angry with him and with me, and still he is so damnably... *civil!*"

Serena laughed. "What a monster the man is."

Frances gave a reluctant smile. "I am unreasonable, I know. But I can't help thinking that if he cared, he would shout at me."

Serena shook her head. "He would not shout at you."

Frances gazed at her in astonishment, waiting for more, but Serena was silent for some time.

"Do you want my advice, Fran?" she said at last.

Frances nodded.

"Seduce him," Serena said bluntly.

"Serena!" Somehow, she was shocked by such words from her little sister, but Serena was married now, too, with a child on the way. "Is that how you get around Tamar?"

"Sometimes," Serena admitted with a quick smile. "It doesn't always work, of course, but it is fun trying."

Frances laughed and climbed to her feet. "I shall bear it in mind. I must go and feed my little monster, but I'll be up in the morning to see you off. Goodnight, Serena."

They embraced, and then Frances hurried off. She went first to Maria's chamber and found her sound asleep. With relief, she moved on to the nursery and discovered her younger sisters in the same condition. Satisfied, and with no further excuse to put it off, she returned to the bedchamber she shared with her husband. A lamp still burned there, illuminating a rather charming vignette.

Torridon was sitting up in bed, bare-chested, and bouncing a grinning, laughing baby on his lap. So much for him screaming at his father.

"Supper has arrived," he told the baby. "I suppose that means I shall be ignored now."

Jamie turned his wobbly head and focused on Frances as she approached the bed. He smiled and returned to gazing at his father.

"Apparently not," she said lightly.

"Not yet," Torridon corrected. "Sit on the bed and I'll unfasten you."

She obeyed, telling herself she couldn't face ringing for a maid at this time. But as he unlaced her gown and her stays, she couldn't help remembering her sister's advice. *Seduce him.*

There were many reasons she did not feel able to try. And yet her body remembered his touch and reacted without permission.

She refused to look at him as she walked across the room, so that her back was to him. She let her clothes drop to the floor and slipped her loose night rail over her head before picking up the fallen garments and tossing them on the chair beside Alan's. He must have dismissed his valet, too.

She turned back to the bed, trying not to stare at his broad, naked shoulders and chest. Why did he not wear a night shirt? His skin looked golden in the lamp light, and in spite of everything, she ached to touch it, stroke it.

Torridon reached out one hand and turned back the covers for her. Without fuss, she walked across the room and climbed in, reaching for the baby with rather more calm than she actually felt.

Jamie gave up his game for his supper quite happily. Stroking his head as she often did while he fed, and gazing into his large, adoring eyes, she was nevertheless very aware of her watching husband. Her night rail was pushed off one shoulder to enable her to feed, and his gaze seemed to burn her naked skin.

Seduce him…

Would she not know then if he loved her?

No, for he would want another heir. That was not love.

"I am a decisive man by nature," he said conversationally. "I commanded men, led them into battle with no doubts as to how and when, and I did it well. And yet in normal life, I flounder. I do not know how to be the Earl of Torridon. I have no idea how to care for a wife and child, and so I have relied on the advice of the woman closest to me who has had children of her own. I forgot such advice could be… colored by many things that have nothing to do with you or me or Jamie. I'm sorry. I should have listened to your instincts and my own."

Slowly, she raised her gaze to his, searching his serious, dark eyes.

He said, "I could not bear to lose you."

Her heartbeat had quickened. She swallowed, trying to calm it. "Why not?" she asked boldly. "There are other women of birth and property who could give you children."

A frown tugged at his brow and vanished. "There is only one you." His eyes were warm, heart-meltingly tender... surely a man could not simulate such emotion?

She tilted her chin. "Does that mean you love me?"

He blinked. "Do you really need to ask that?" he said hoarsely.

"Yes."

His eyes widened. Slowly, he reached out and touched her cheek, letting the backs of his fingers trail down to her lips. "Then yes, I love you. Everyone but you knows I have always loved you."

Warm blood seeped into her face. She didn't know whether to laugh or cry, but some intense, powerful emotion seemed to be trying to burst out of her.

"Perhaps you *told* everyone but me," she managed.

"I am not good with words," he said ruefully. "I am too practical. But I do learn from my mistakes, and I will win you again." Despite Jamie's presence, he leaned over and kissed her lips.

Butterflies soared in her stomach. And this time she opened her mouth for him, let her lips cling to his as they wanted. She had been won by his kisses long ago, but she had forgotten the sheer, physical sweetness...

Jamie detached himself from her breast and squawked in protest at being squashed between them. They broke apart, laughing a little breathlessly at his peremptory ways. But his eyes were already closed, drifting into sleep. Frances rose and padded across to the dressing room, which had been turned into a temporary nursery. He didn't make a sound as she laid him in the cradle and covered him.

Then, with a sense of deep anticipation, she walked back into the bedchamber. Torridon watched her, appreciative, almost predatory. And when she slid back into bed, sitting beside him against the propped-up pillows, he turned and took both her hands, raising them to his lips one after the other before he again kissed her mouth.

"I had almost forgotten how soft and sweet you are," he whispered against her lips. "And yet I dreamed of you nearly every night."

She slid her hands over his warm shoulders, wondering if she was silly to give in so easily. Only she had longed for his embrace so much.

She pressed her cheek against his. "I missed you," she gasped into his ear. "If I behaved badly—and I know I did—it's because I missed *you.*"

"I know. Shall we start again?"

She smiled into his neck, inhaling the scent of his skin. "You mean, wait to be introduced and dance together, make stilted conversation in public?"

"Your conversation was never stilted."

"Neither was yours." He had been magnificent, confident, charming, making her laugh and overwhelming her with sheer emotion that she had been too innocent to put a name to.

Now she knew it as desire, lusts of the flesh, and it was happening all over again. She began to tremble as he kissed his way down her throat to the neckline of her nightgown. She stroked his back, smoothing her palms over the rippling muscle, remembering with familiar pleasure and new wonder.

His mouth found hers once more, kissing her deeply, while he drew her down to lie beside him, half under him. His hardness pressed urgently against her thigh. Her whole being ached for his love.

He groaned softly into her mouth. "Good night, my sweet," he whispered and lay back on the pillows.

Stunned, aching, she took a moment to turn her back on him and douse the lamp. She didn't know whether she felt more hurt or frustrated.

Seduce him, Serena had said. Well, that clearly didn't work.

He moved, clasping her shoulder as he loomed over her again.

"Just to be sure you know," he murmured, "this is harder for me."

"Then why—" she began and broke off with a jerk of impatience. She refused to ask.

Of course, he understood anyhow. "Because we are starting again," he reminded her. "And it is not gentlemanly to seduce a gentlewoman on the first night of one's acquaintance."

She didn't know whether to laugh or slap him. "And where did you discover this little-known point of etiquette?" she managed.

"Oh, I read it in a book somewhere. But I give you notice, on the second day, you are fair game."

In spite of herself, she shivered with anticipation. "Unless, left to myself, I rediscover my shyness."

He settled down at her back, wrapping his warm, completely naked body around hers. His smiling lips brushed her neck. "I look forward to breaking down that barrier. If I find it."

Happier than she had been for months, Frances closed her eyes and wallowed in her husband's embrace. It had been a long time since she had looked forward to the next day. Suddenly, life was full of exciting possibilities once more. Of warmth and gladness and love.

Chapter Thirteen

DAYLIGHT STREAMED THROUGH the curtains they had never closed. Sounds of bustle came from inside the castle and out. Carriages were being loaded, ready for Serena's departure.

Frances was aware at once of her husband's presence in her bed. His hand brushed the side of her knee, where her night rail had got caught up in sleep, and unhurriedly caressed its way up her leg to thigh and hip. Slow-burning desire weighed down her limbs, but since she had no wish to move, that hardly mattered. Alan was here with her at last, his hand continuing its slow, sensual journey under her nightgown to her waist and upward until it found the soft curve of her breast.

She turned her head toward him, reaching for his kiss. He gave it, and the sweet ache in her body caught fire. A low, excited breath of laughter escaped him, because he knew she was won. As she always was.

But she was no longer a naïve, wide-eyed girl. And she would not let her love, her physical surrender be taken for granted ever again.

Detaching her lips from his, with some difficulty, she said breathlessly, "Not now, my lord."

He smiled, pulling her under him. His hardness pressed between her thighs. "My book of etiquette is quite clear that this morning is quite permissible."

"That must be the gentlemen's book. The ladies' book says not."

"Does it give reasons?"

"Oh, yes. In short, I am too busy. Jamie will wake momentarily,

T H E   W I C K E D   W I F E

and my sister is preparing to leave."

"If I know Serena, she will be preparing for some time." His wicked hand continued its caresses.

It was one of the hardest things she had ever done, to lie still and not throw her arms around him in abandonment. Her whole body was aflame. Perhaps he knew very well that a little more perseverance would reduce her to a pliable blob of lust. She couldn't take the chance.

Reluctantly, but firmly, she pushed his shoulders and turned him on to his back. He went willingly, as though he thought it part of her love-play, but without his weight upon her, she slid out of his arms and the bed.

He laughed softly. "Minx."

Smiling, she checked on Jamie who still slumbered peacefully, and went in search of clothes. Torridon lay propped up on pillows, his hands behind his head, watching her every move as she washed and dressed. And that was exciting, too.

"Come here," he growled, low, when she was brushing her hair.

But as she turned to him, Jamie woke with a demanding cry. And so, while she fed the baby, Torridon appeared to give up, rising to wash and dress himself.

Frances had little to compare his body to, but the sight of Torridon without clothes had always overwhelmed her with awe and desire. She ached to relearn its every plane and muscle and hard curve. She wanted to hold him, feel him moving on her, within her.

Swallowing, she returned her attention to Jamie.

After a while, as other matters flitted through her mind, she said, "You have been here a few days now. Did you see much of my little sisters? Maria in particular?"

"Not really. The castle was full of guests. Why?"

"Maria has an admirer, a young officer whom she meets in secret. It is innocent, of course, for the moment, although the world will not necessarily believe that. I spoke to her yesterday, but I have a feeling the matter is not over. I just wondered if you or anyone else had

141

noticed her unhappiness."

Torridon patted himself dry with a towel. "No one has mentioned it in my hearing. And I'm afraid I have been too involved in my own business to notice hers. Who is the man concerned? Does Braithwaite not like him?"

"I doubt Braithwaite has ever met him," Frances said wryly. "He was the officer you struck the night of the ball."

Torridon paused with his shirt half over his head, staring at her. "That is not good. But did Maria not see him in that state? Did it not cure her infatuation?" He straightened the shirt, and reached for his pantaloons.

"It certainly gave her pause. He disappointed her quite gravely." Frances sighed. "However, I fear she may be a little like me. If she feels she has made a commitment, she may well feel obliged to stick to it beyond what is reasonable."

For an instant, Torridon met her gaze, his eyes oddly stricken. Too late, she realized he had taken the comparison to mean her commitment to him was a matter of obligation. In reality, she had been thinking of her unreasonable commitment to the wager with Ariadne.

His eyelids swept down, hiding the emotion. Frances opened her mouth to explain, but Jamie, replete for the time being, let out a squawk, and by the time she turned him onto her shoulder to wind him, Torridon had begun to speak of other things.

As if the awkward moment had never been, he obligingly fastened her gown for her. And then, with a quick smile, she left him, taking the baby with her as she went in search of Serena.

TORRIDON WATCHED HER go. He couldn't deny that the comparison of her commitment with Maria's had wounded him. But, in fact, it didn't make sense. The fog of doubts and suspicions and sheer anger that had haunted him since she'd fled Torridon had vanished. He now had a much clearer view of his passionate, loyal wife whom he himself had unwittingly made unhappy. If she had ever stuck to her commitment through mere obligation, he should be grateful. But in his heart, he didn't think she ever had. The love he had sensed had always been there. She had been talking of something else... her wager with Ariadne Marshall, no doubt.

Either way, he would not let it cloud his day or interfere with his courtship. And he knew perfectly well what she had been doing this morning—paying him back for his abstinence last night. But he would not take her again merely as a matter of course. This time there had to be a clear understanding between them. He had to win her utterly, completely.

Still, her teasing this morning enflamed him even further, for he relished the hunt and anticipated the end result with ever-greater pleasure. He might have still chastised himself for a blind fool who had unwittingly hurt her and all but wrecked their marriage, but he no longer doubted her love or his ability to hold her. To take her when he chose, with her full, delightful cooperation. Oh yes...

Adjusting his pantaloons, he reached for his boots. His valet arrived and was sent away with nothing to do, and Torridon strolled off to inspect the chaos of the Tamars' departure.

Three coaches waited at the front door, two crammed with baggage. More was being brought out constantly and being bestowed either inside or on the roofs. Serena flitted busily in and out, as did various familiar castle servants and men probably hired for the journey. Or they could have been Braithwaite's retainers, for he travelled to and from London a great deal.

Tamar leaned one shoulder against the wall and seemed to be drawing in a little book held in the palm of his hand. Torridon strolled up to him and examined the amusing sketch of people rushing to fill a coach that was buckling under the weight, while an attached horse had turned its head to watch with an expression of horror.

Torridon laughed, and Tamar grinned in response.

"Is any of that stuff actually yours?" Torridon asked.

"One small trunk. And some painting gear. But most of that was in my studio—been sent ahead already. I think your wife is trying to persuade mine to leave behind her bedchamber furniture and gowns she had when she was fourteen years old." He straightened, stuffing the notebook and pencil into his pocket. "It's hard for her to leave. Perhaps it would have been easier if we'd gone as soon as we were married."

Torridon considered. "No. You know each other better now, and so the change in scene will be easier for her with that support. Besides, she'll thoroughly enjoy arranging everything. She loves a project, Frances tells me."

"Well, she's already taken Sylvester in hand," Tamar observed as his brother emerged carrying two framed pictures and a Queen Anne chair. "After that, a ruined house and estate will seem like a stroll in the park. How the devil are they going to get the chair in?"

"Roof," Torridon said succinctly. "Good luck, my friend!"

He had caught sight of Maria in a voluminous cloak, her expression unhappy as she stood alone behind the coaches, watching the proceedings. He strolled up to her, which seemed to surprise her, although she summoned up a wan smile.

"Have you given up on Serena's packing?" he asked lightly.

"She has Frances."

"From what I hear, she needs a small army just to persuade her to leave the castle furniture."

"Life is changing for her again. For all of us," Maria remarked. It didn't appear to fill her with pleasure. She glanced to the left, toward the woods.

"Doesn't it always?" Torridon said.

"No. For years it stays the same."

"No it doesn't," Torridon argued. "It just changes more slowly. I hear you are coming to stay with us."

"Perhaps," Maria replied vaguely. "Later… if you'll have me."

"Of course we will," Torridon said.

Again, she glanced toward the woods. She was tense, strung as tightly as a bow, like a soldier before battle. At least he knew how to help with that.

"Walk with me a little," he invited, turning in the direction she kept looking.

Maria hesitated a moment, then fell into step beside him.

"Frances is worried about you," he said. "She thinks you are unhappy."

Maria laughed, presumably by way of proof to the contrary. "And what do you think?"

"That she's right. And that you look like someone who's about to do something they don't want to do."

"I don't know what you mean."

"I used to command men in battle. I saw many soldiers, and not just the untried ones, determined to do their duty and fight when what they really wanted to do was stay exactly where they were—or preferably run back to their homes and families."

"But they fought anyway," Maria guessed, looking at him. "They did their duty."

"Their duty was clear cut in those cases, though sometimes they had to be talked into it. Other duties are not so obvious. Like yours at this moment."

Her eyes widened. "You mean I should be with Serena?"

"I think you *wish* to be with Serena."

"Perhaps."

"But for some reason, you believe your duty is elsewhere."

Her breath caught. Then she laughed again, a short, mirthless sound. "Would you believe me if I said I am about to elope with the man you hit the night of the ball?"

"No," Torridon said calmly. "I don't believe you are so silly. I think you are contemplating it with considerably less joy than is necessary for such a step, but won't bring yourself to do it."

"And yet, he's waiting for me now, in a borrowed curricle on the road beyond these trees."

"And you told him you would go?"

She nodded dumbly. "I suppose you will tell Frances and Mama and Gervaise."

"And we will all rush to stop you? Is that why you're telling me?"

"I don't know why I'm telling you. Won't you though? Rush to stop me?"

He considered. "I don't think I need to rush. But yes, I will stop you."

"Why?" she whispered.

"Because there is nothing but misery for you with him. And here, with your family, you have such a bright future. It's not your reputation they would mourn, Maria. It's your happiness. Do you not know how much they love you?"

"I don't know anything anymore," she whispered. She dashed the back of her hand across her eyes. "Except that you're right—I don't want to go with him. And yet…"

"And yet you feel you should since you've said you would."

She nodded. "You must think me very stupid."

"No." He didn't elaborate. Instead he said, "I think we should both go to meet your ardent suitor. Don't worry, I shan't hit him again unless he insults you. Tell him how you feel while I am there to protect you. If he is half a gentleman, he will be ashamed of himself. Or if you prefer, I will play the heavy-handed brother and forbid him from seeing you again. Don't worry, he will obey."

Maria shivered. "You can be quite frightening, can't you?"

"To foolish or badly-behaved young soldiers? Oh yes."

A flicker of humor lit her unhappy eyes. She drew in a breath. "I think I should be honest with him, don't you? He deserves that much."

Torridon didn't believe the bounder deserved anything but a severe kick in the breeches. But he merely inclined his head.

Maria swallowed. "I would be grateful for your company."

"I'm afraid you have to have that, grateful or not. Come, let us hurry so it is done, and you can be back in time to say goodbye to Serena."

This time, her smile was better, and a few minutes later, he glimpsed a waiting curricle through the trees. Her tension redoubled, raising her shoulders noticeably inside the cloak. Torridon bit back the platitudes about him not being worth her pain, or that if he truly loved her he would wait. He suspected it was the loss of love she was mourning, not the loss of her soldier. As he recalled, though only faintly through the years, there was pain enough in that.

Voices reached them through the trees. Torridon glanced quizzically at Maria, who only shrugged. Eventually, he saw that there were two young men in the curricle, apparently arguing. One was the young officer he had struck, though now in civilian dress. The other was a complete stranger to Torridon.

"Who is with him?" he murmured.

"Bernard," Maria said blankly. "It's Bernard Muir, Gillie's brother. Lady Wickenden's brother," she corrected herself. And it seemed that the presence of a childhood friend made the whole scene more natural. She actually increased her speed, calling, "Bernard? What in the world are you doing here?"

Both heads jerked up to face her, taking in not only her presence but Torridon's, too. The officer's face blanched. Involuntarily, he touched the bruise on his cheek.

The other young man seemed not in the slightest put out. "Maria," he said in a business-like manner, jumping down from the curricle. "That is, *Lady* Maria," he added with another quick glance at Torridon. "I've lent Heath my curricle, but only so I could drive him up here to speak to you. No idea who you are, sir, but if you haven't come to forbid this—which I hope you have—I wish you'd talk some sense into these two."

"Why, Bernard," Maria said on a choke of laughter that was almost a sob. "Have you come to save my honor?"

"Not sure *exactly* why I came," Bernard admitted. "Except that Heath seemed to think I was the most respectable of his friends— which says a lot, in my opinion!—and I should lend him my new curricle to elope with you. Anyway, the question is, Maria, what do *you* want? Do you actually want to go to Scotland and leg-shackle yourself to this gudgeon?"

The officer scowled at his so-called friend, who clearly wasn't behaving as expected.

Maria, pale now, looked from Bernard to Heath and then hurriedly to Torridon.

"It's a good question," Torridon said quietly. "And one that should be answered before all the others."

Maria swallowed and turned her gaze back on Lieutenant Heath, who hadn't even stepped down from the curricle. He seemed to be frozen in his seat, his appalled gaze hovering between Maria and Torridon.

"No," Maria whispered. Then, in a stronger voice, she continued. "No, I don't want to go with him. I'm sorry, Gideon. I have misled myself as well as you, but I don't wish to marry you. In fact, I should have stuck with what I said the day after the ball. I don't want to see you again. Whatever was between us is over."

Heath's Adam's apple wobbled. He nodded once, seeming more anxious to get away from this situation than to elope. He didn't even try to persuade her otherwise.

"Thank God that's settled," Bernard said in some relief. "I told you how it would be, Heath. She's too young and she's not for you. Even if she wasn't the earl's sister, she's not for you. I'm going back to Blackhaven..." He glanced at Maria. "Unless I can drive you to the castle first?"

Maria shook her head a little wildly and grasped Torridon's arm. "Oh no. I'll walk back with Lord Torridon."

"Oh, *that's* who you are!" Bernard exclaimed, thrusting out his hand. "I'm Bernard Muir, Lady Wickenden's brother. Very glad to make your acquaintance, sir."

Torridon took his hand. "I believe I'm glad to make yours."

Bernard grinned, then scuffed his foot a little awkwardly on the road. "I take it we're in agreement on the subject of discretion?"

"You may rely on me," Torridon said gravely.

Bernard grinned again. "Had to ask," he said cheerfully and climbed on to the curricle, gathering the ribbons. Heath sat staring straight ahead.

"Bernard," Maria said. "Thank you."

Bernard saluted her with his whip.

"One more thing," Torridon said. "Lieutenant Heath."

The officer jerked his head around in alarm.

"Lady Maria has made her wishes plain." Torridon said sternly. "If you do more than bow to her from a distance or even mention her name, I will know."

Heath nodded curtly and muttered something to Bernard. He didn't even look at Maria as the curricle set off in the direction of Blackhaven.

"How do you feel?" Torridon murmured, gazing after it.

"As if a huge weight has fallen from my shoulders. And yet I want to cry. He wasn't what I thought, and neither am I."

"Then I think," he said thoughtfully, "that we should race back to the castle. Serena may surprise us yet with her own burst of speed." With that he took off, loping through the trees. After a startled moment, she laughed and her feet pounded behind him. He grinned. "Can't catch me."

"Can I not?" she said at once.

Chapter Fourteen

T HE RACE THROUGH the woods with Maria got them back to the castle quickly. It also gave Maria the opportunity to run off her immediate blue-devils and face her family with greater ease of mind. Then, together, they entered the old part of the castle, following the trail of servants to the Tamars' rooms in the old part of the castle.

"No, Serena," Frances was saying firmly. "You can't take the escritoire. Strictly speaking, it isn't yours, it's Gervaise and Eleanor's." She stood in the middle of the room beside Serena while the younger girls perched on the bed looking morose.

Serena seemed inclined to argue. "Gervaise told me years ago that I could count all of this mine."

"Isn't there any furniture in Tamar Abbey?" Frances asked.

"Not much, though Tamar says our own rooms are habitable—"

"Then that will include a desk, probably a much finer one than that old thing. Keep it here for when you visit."

Torridon smiled to himself as Serena was persuaded. She even gave a reluctant laugh.

"I'm being a little ridiculous, aren't I?" she said.

Torridon moved aside to let the last of the servants out with the bags containing the Tamars' things that they would need for stopovers during the various nights of their journey.

"Yes," Frances admitted, casting a quick smile of welcome to Torridon and Maria. It did his heart good. "But never mind. You will soon be so busy that you won't have time to miss the castle. After all, you never did when you came to London."

"That is very true." Serena seized her travelling cloak. "Come and wave us off then. Girls, do you have shawls or cloaks with you?"

"I don't," Frances remembered.

"I'll fetch it," Torridon said and, leaving Maria with her sisters, he strode off back into the main part of the castle and across the landing to the passage leading to his and Frances's bedchamber.

Ahead, he saw one of the carrying servants coming out of their rooms and walking on, presumably to the nearest side-door. The man was clearly empty-handed, so he must have been delivering something from Serena's room to Frances, which wasn't entirely unexpected. But he found himself focusing on the figure hurrying away from him. Something was odd about the man, something he couldn't put his finger on.

Not that it mattered. He found his wife's shawl easily enough and hurried downstairs and back outside where the final farewells were being said. Serena thoroughly embraced everyone, including Torridon, with special hugs for her little sisters. Maria clung to her a little too hard, but managed to smile.

Tamar and his young brother were much more casual, although Tamar himself said something clearly serious to Braithwaite as they shook hands. Braithwaite smiled and clapped him on the back.

"Just take care of her, and invite us to stay," he said.

Frances, after hugging Serena one last time came to stand by Torridon, her hand on Helen's shoulder as the girls stood on the step below, waving dementedly.

The burdened cavalcade set off with its outriders, and everyone called goodbye and good luck messages after it. The girls would have run after it, but Gervaise and Frances held them back in case they got in the way of the horses.

"Don't cry, Helen," Frances said, squeezing the child's shoulder. "It's just like a big adventure for Serena, and you will see her and Tamar before you know it."

Adventure, Torridon thought. For some reason, the word made him remember Frances in boy's clothes, swaggering into the tavern…

and quite abruptly, he knew what had been "wrong" about the servant coming out of their bedchamber only minutes ago. He hadn't moved like a man. His rear hadn't been a man's. It had been rounded like a woman's and it had rolled slightly in walking.

A woman dressed as a man coming out of Frances's bedchamber. *Ariadne Marshall.*

No. It couldn't be. Without a word, he turned and bolted back into the house. He all but ran across the hall and took the stairs three at a time, rushing to the bedchamber.

He had watched Frances bestow the rubies in her dressing table drawer. Yanking it open, he was thoroughly relieved to see the jewel case still there. Still, something made him open it just to be sure.

The rubies were gone.

"God damn it," he fumed, slamming the drawer. Was that woman never content but with the last word? Seizing his overcoat and hat, he charged out of the room once more. On the stairs, he met Frances. "Have to rush! Back as soon as I can!" he said, dashing past her.

But she wasn't having that. "Alan!" She flew back down the stairs after him, seizing his arm to make him halt. "Where are you going?"

"After the rubies," he said impatiently. "They've been stolen."

She blinked. "Again?"

For some reason, it made him laugh. "Sadly, yes, and she's—the thief is getting away."

She pounced on his slip. "She? Who?"

He had tried. There was no point now. "Ariadne Marshall," he said reluctantly.

Her eyes widened. "Ari? *Ari?*" Her jaw dropped and snapped shut. She didn't accuse him of obsessive hatred or even being mistaken. "Ariadne stole from me." Her eyes refocused on his. "She took them the last time, too, didn't she? That's how you got them back. You took them back from her somehow, once you realized I had lost them. Why didn't you tell me?"

He touched her cheek. "I didn't want you to be wounded by her perfidy. I thought I would simply send her away."

Unexpectedly, Frances caught his hand and held it there for an instant. "You are rather wonderful," she whispered. She dropped his hand, scowling. "Ariadne never leaves a game alone. You *can't* send her away. Order the carriage, Torridon; I'm coming with you."

"No need," he called after her. "I'll be quicker riding in any case."

"But you don't know where she is!" Frances flung over her shoulder. "I know the country and I know Ariadne!"

He was bound to admit that was true, and so he ordered his own carriage instead of one of Braithwaite's more sporting vehicles. He also begged the use of one of Braithwaite's under-coachmen who also knew the country well. And he was glad he did, for as the carriage halted at the front steps and he strode toward it, Frances ran out of the house with Jamie in one arm, and a bag in the other.

"SHE'LL BE AT The Black Lion in Whalen," Frances told her husband as the carriage set off at a smart pace. "There's no other hostelry outside Blackhaven that she would tolerate."

That Ariadne had stolen from her, not once but twice, stunned Frances. Below her calm and determination bubbled a cauldron of indignation, hurt, and shame. She had been foolish. But what really roused her ire was that Ariadne now dared to conduct this war with her husband.

"If my friendship truly mattered to her, she would not have done this," Frances said flatly.

"I suspect she imagined I would not tell you," Torridon said, "that despite my threats, I would keep her crimes to myself."

"Why didn't you?" Frances asked curiously.

Torridon shrugged. "There has been enough silence between us," he muttered. "Enough unsaid."

She covered his hand resting on the seat between them. "I do not need to be protected from honesty. Of any kind."

His hand turned, and he threaded his fingers through hers. "I know."

Jamie stared at the windows, watching the changing scenery flit by, fields and woods, and moors on one side, the sea on the other. The sea was tranquil today, a bright, glassy blue in the spring sunshine. Eventually, they trundled into Whalen, the carriage negotiating its bustling, muddy streets. It was not as clean or as genteel as Black-haven. Whalen was a working town, the largest in the area until Blackhaven had begun to grow into the fashionable spa town it now was.

Frances's heartbeat quickened as the carriage stopped, and Torri-don handed her out. She had no idea what she would say to Ariadne, if she could even bear to look at her. But she did want to stand by her husband's side and confront her.

"Alan, how important are the rubies to you?" she asked suddenly. They had originally been acquired by his great-great-grandfather, the third earl, who had presented them to his countess on their wedding day. They were part of the estate, a symbol of the Torridon name, wealth, and honor. To steal them was an insult to his family. Or at least she expected him to say something similar.

"I gave them to you," he said shortly. "Not to her."

She gazed at him in surprise, warmed by his answer and yet more curious than ever. But she had to contain her questions, for by then they had entered the inn and Torridon asked peremptorily for Mrs. Marshall.

"Oh, the lady left, sir, not a quarter of an hour since."

"Thank you!" Frances seized her husband's arm before he could ask more questions and all but dragged him toward the door. "She's going south," she said urgently. "We'll catch her."

Torridon was about to hand her into the carriage, when a familiar figure suddenly bolted out of the inn. "My lady, my lady!"

"Lawson?" Frances said in disbelief, turning to face the maid who was rushing across the yard with her cap askew. "Is Mrs. Marshall here after all?"

Lawson slid to a halt in front of her, already smiling at Jamie, who smiled back as if he remembered her. "No, my lady, but she's riding—alone—and I'm to make my own way to London. But when I saw you and his little lordship..."

"Lawson is Mrs. Marshall's abigail," Frances told her husband, and the maid remembered to curtsey speedily, her attention still more than half on the baby. "She was most helpful caring for Jamie. How are you supposed to get to London?"

"On the stagecoach, my lady. It stops here tomorrow morning."

But Torridon had focused on the other half of Lawson's news. "She's riding alone all the way to London?" he said in disbelief. "That would be ruinous, not to say downright dangerous."

"She is reckless," Frances allowed, frowning, "but by no means foolish. Lawson, has she gone to meet someone? Please tell me it is not Lord Sylvester Gaunt!"

"I don't know who it is," Lawson said reluctantly, "but I'm fairly sure she wouldn't go far alone. And if she is planning to meet someone, she doesn't want me there."

Frances's frown deepened, "But you know all her secrets, don't you? Why would she keep this from you?"

"Because she's planning to let me go, probably," Lawson said morosely. "At least she paid my fare to London, where I'm more likely to find another position."

"Lawson..." Frances fixed the maid with her kindliest gaze. "I shan't be angry, but did you know she had stolen my rubies?"

Lawson's eyes widened. "I thought you were wagering them!" She cast a half-frightened glance at Torridon's stern figure. "Begging your pardon. But no, I had no idea she took them... wait, though, I did see an extra jewel case in her drawer. I thought it was a gift from the young lord who... er... called."

"That particular young lord has less chance of buying rubies than you do," Frances said wryly.

"Oh. In any case, I didn't look inside. Mrs. Marshall cares for her own jewels. Such as she has left." A troubled, mortified look filled her face. "I'm glad I didn't know. I've always been loyal to my ladies, scrupulously loyal, but I can't hold with stealing, my lady, and most certainly not from you! And you were so upset! What you went through to find them... and she let you! I couldn't have kept quiet, my lady, I couldn't!"

While Frances patted the agitated maid's shoulder, Torridon asked, "Which direction did she take?"

"South, sir, along the coast road."

"Then I suggest we look for her," Torridon said briskly, and urged Frances into the carriage.

"Begging your pardon, my lord, my lady," Lawson burst out. "Can I come, too? I have a piece of my mind to deliver to madam! Along with my resignation."

"By all means," Torridon said politely. "Join the party."

ONLY A FEW miles outside Whalen was a fork in the road, with one way leading inland across the moors. Since Ariadne had been so focused on going to London, Frances was at first happy to carry on along the coast road, until they stopped and inquired of an old couple walking if they had seen a lady riding in this direction. They denied seeing anything except a farmer's gig and a brewer's cart.

"She could have ridden out of their sight," Frances said.

"Why would she bother?" Torridon argued. "Their notice would mean nothing to her. But what would attract her along the other road? Is there another inn to stop for the night?"

"None that would be safe for her to stay alone," Frances said. "There is The Crown, but I doubt she would reach it before dark." She thought. "There are a couple of villages, a scattering of gentlemen's houses... oh, and an old ruined church that Serena and I always thought was haunted. We rode there a few times with Gervaise."

"I don't suppose you mentioned this to Ariadne?"

Frances frowned. "I might have," she said doubtfully. "But a ruined church doesn't meet her minimal standard of comfort."

"But it might as a mere meeting point," Torridon said, and stuck his head out of the door to instruct the driver to turn, a tricky maneuver without spilling coach and occupants in the ditch. "We don't need to go far along the road, just until we discover if anyone has seen her. If no one has, we'll come back to the coast road."

Since this seemed a sensible course, the coachman was instructed to halt and make inquiries of the first person he saw.

"Do you have somewhere to stay in London while you look for a new position?" Frances asked Lawson.

"I expect I can stay with my sister for a few days," Lawson replied. She raised her eyes from her folded hands. "I tried my best with Mrs. Marshall," she burst out, "but I just wasn't comfortable with her ways. I know you and she got up to mischief together, but you were never less than a lady. Mrs. Marshall... all those men and secret letters and staying out all night. I'd rather not have to deal with such things!"

"I'm sure you'll be able to choose from any number of respectable positions," Frances soothed. "And then—" She clung onto the seat as the coach slowed too suddenly. Lawson was flung off on to the floor. Torridon leaned forward, reaching for her as the carriage came to an abrupt halt amidst the sound of snorting, stamping horses. Presumably, the coachman had found someone to question.

A male voice outside could be heard saying, "Don't."

Torridon, abandoning Lawson on the floor, leaned back and reached into the velvet pocket by the window.

"Don't," repeated the man who opened the carriage door at the same time. He wore a hat pulled low over his brow, and a neckerchief had been drawn up over the bottom half of his face. More importantly, he held a pistol in either hand.

Frances gasped. Lawson scuttled under her seat. Torridon took his hand from the velvet pocket without the pistol that was kept there.

"Good man," the highwayman pronounced in a broad Scottish accent. "Now if you would both please step down into the road, I shall relieve you of your valuables. No heroics, if you please, sir. I'd hate your wife and bairn to be hurt."

Torridon grasped Frances's hand, his grip strong and soothing. Without even glancing in Lawson's direction, he got down first and helped Frances. Jamie slept peacefully on. The coachman, looking grim, was ordered down beside them.

"Empty your pockets, then!" the highwayman commanded. "Purses and jewels are my favorites. Thank you, ma'am," he added, retrieving Frances's reticule from her numb wrist.

Under her fascinated gaze—she had never been held up before—he inspected the contents, grunting with dissatisfaction. "No jewels?"

Torridon laughed, which surprised a smile to her lips. The highwayman, of course, didn't understand the joke. With a tut of annoyance, he stuffed the whole bag inside his coat. Torridon's pockets pleased him more.

"Very good," he pronounced, dropping all the bank notes and coins into his own capacious pocket.

"That," Torridon said, "is the worst Scottish accent I have ever heard."

"It is," the highwayman agreed. "But it serves its purpose. What's in the bag?"

Frances tensed as he reached into the coach and brought out the bag full of Jamie's things and rummaged through the shawls, cleaning cloths, napkins, and the baby's favorite rattle.

Clearly disgusted, the highwayman threw the bag back inside. "I'd have expected you to travel with servants and jewel boxes," he complained.

"My apologies," Torridon said. "They must have fallen off the roof rack."

The highwayman let out a cackle of laughter. "Aye, you're a funny man, and in other circumstances I'd enjoy a dram with you. You. Master coachman, be so good as to tie my horse to the carriage."

Mark the under-coachman scowled. "Tie him yourself."

"Well, I will if you like, but I'd have to shoot one of you to keep the upper hand."

"Do it," Torridon ordered.

Mark obeyed. It dawned on Frances belatedly that the highwayman was now stealing the entire carriage, and that poor Lawson was still inside it. She started forward in alarm, but Torridon held onto her hand with a warning squeeze.

The highwayman then pocketed one pistol, and touched the barrel of the other to his hat in a jaunty salute before clambering up onto the box. "Ya!" he said, and the horses broke into an almost instant gallop.

"Oh dear, poor Lawson," Frances said anxiously. "She'll be thrown around horrendously! What if he kills her?"

"He won't," Torridon assured her. "He's just making sure we can't call the authorities on him too quickly. He'll abandon the carriage somewhere, and Lawson will simply walk away—hopefully sending help back to us."

Frances groaned. "But this is so annoying! I own it's exciting to be held up by such an amiable highwayman, but not when we're in such a hurry looking for Ariadne. This is *such* bad luck!"

"It is," Torridon agreed thoughtfully. "Astoundingly bad, in fact." He took Jamie from her, settling him in the crook of one arm, while he offered the other to Frances. They might have been strolling in the park. "What if Ariadne somehow discovered we were following her? And the highwayman is the man she is going to meet?"

Frances's eyes widened. "Ari and a *highwayman*? You mean she sent him just to slow us up?"

"Possibly."

"Then we must be on the right road." Frances increased her pace. "We must hurry!"

WITH THE ABRUPT departure of the Torridons on some unspecified expedition, and her mother-in-law's decision to take her younger daughters into Blackhaven, Eleanor, or Dawn as she still tended to think of herself, found the castle suddenly empty. If one didn't count the small army of servants. Nevertheless, she was able to entice her husband out of his library to enjoy a couple of hours of secret pleasure in their bedchamber.

Gervaise was more than happy to linger. In fact, when they were interrupted by his valet in the outer chamber, he was inclined to wrath.

"I have been asked to tell you, my lord, that Lady Torridon has called," the valet said woodenly. "Her ladyship awaits your pleasure in the small drawing room."

Gervaise scowled at the closed door. "Frances can look after herself. What does he mean—"

"Not Frances," Dawn said, springing up. "It must be Torridon's mother!"

"His mother? What the devil is she doing here? Did you invite her? Did Frances?"

"Lord, no." Dawn slid out of bed and reached for her carelessly discarded clothes. "If you ask me, she is a large part of Frances's problem. This might be an opportunity to negotiate peace."

However, when Dawn walked into the drawing room, she knew at once that the lady would not be easily placated.

"Lady Torridon," she greeted her uninvited guest, advancing with her hand held out. "What a pleasure to meet you. I'm so sorry to keep you waiting."

"No apology is necessary," Lady Torridon said graciously. "It is I who must apologize for the intrusion. To be frank, Lady Braithwaite, I am looking for son or my daughter-in-law, or my grandson. Are any of them here with you?"

"All of them," Dawn replied. "That is, they are all staying here, but they have gone off on an expedition."

Lady Torridon narrowed her eyes. "Together?"

"Yes, baby and all."

"And that woman, Mrs. Marshall?"

Dawn blinked. "I don't believe I know a Mrs. Marshall. She is certainly not staying here. But please, sit and let me ring for tea. You must wait for them, of course."

Lady Torridon sat, her back ramrod-straight.

Dawn took a chair next to her. "Forgive me, ma'am, but is something wrong?"

Lady Torridon brushed the back of her gloved hand over her forehead. "Wrong? Where do I begin? My daughter-in-law has not been... well, not since the birth of my grandson. She is moody and erratic... the last straw was when she fled her home without a word, taking my grandson with her, lying, hiding... in short, I fear for my grandson's safety."

With an effort, Dawn picked up her dropped jaw. "You will be glad to know I have seen no such signs in Lady Frances. And she takes excellent care of little Jamie. But you must speak to my husband, who obviously knows her much better than I."

Gervaise strolled into the room and bowed to Lady Torridon. "How do you do, Lady Torridon? A pleasure to meet you again."

"I wish it were in happier circumstances," her ladyship said heavily. Clearly, she was not intimidated by Braithwaite and would happily repeat her bizarre accusations against his sister. Dawn regarded him warily.

"What on earth is the matter?" he asked at once.

Lady Torridon sighed. "I gather my son and my daughter-in-law did not arrive here together?"

"No," Braithwaite said, amused, "they did not. But in fashionable society ma'am, it is rare to find married couples in the same house for very long."

"Fiddle-faddle," snapped her ladyship. "It is my belief your sister fled her husband's roof in the company of that woman, Mrs. Marshall, and plans to keep my grandson from Torridon."

Braithwaite blinked. "If such a nonsensical thought ever entered Frances's head, she's making a very poor show of it. Frances and Jamie arrived here in Torridon's company and they've all gone off together this morning. You have it quite wrong if you imagine he is pursuing his errant wife. I witnessed their departure this morning, and Torridon was about to set off alone before Frances came running after him with

Jamie. They left together, so far as I could tell, in perfect harmony with one another."

It was gently spoken and civil, but Lady Torridon was a fool if she did not see the ice behind his eyes. He would allow no one to traduce his sister, and Dawn could not blame him.

"Of course, you are an honorable man and she is your sister," Lady Torridon pronounced. "You are bound to defend her, and it is not my desire to give you pain. But I, too, must do what is right, and I tell you now it is my intention to return to Scotland with Jamie as soon as may be, and to keep Frances away from him. With all the weight of the law behind me."

Chapter Fifteen

L AWSON'S ONE FEAR as the carriage careened along the road, was that the highwayman would overturn the vehicle and drop them in the ditch. At least they weren't on the coast road and liable to go over the cliff. Braced against the back of the coach and under the seat, she wasn't too badly bumped. She spent most of the short journey being grateful that the villain hadn't shot the baby or Lady Torridon. What sort of a monster pointed a pistol at a baby? A man with no conscience and no feelings. Which didn't really bode well for her if she was discovered.

In the meantime, she paid attention to the vehicle's direction, noticed when it turned left, and then a few moments later, left again. For one horrible moment, as the carriage finally came to a halt, she was afraid they had come to some terrible thieves' den. But then she heard the clink of glasses and crockery and the tone of laughter told her it was just a tavern, or an inn perhaps.

The latter it seemed. The coach swayed as the highwayman climbed down. "See to the horses, will you?" he said casually. "Just some water and some hay to keep them sweet."

Lawson lay where she was, unable to believe her luck. The highwayman actually began to hum a merry tune to himself as he walked away. For a moment, the humming seemed oddly familiar to her, but then she found most humming equally irritating.

She waited while water and hay was brought for the horses. Ideally, they should have a good long rest after such a gallop, but Lawson was afraid of the highwayman returning. So, she waited only five minutes or so after the stable lads had left, and then, slowly emerged from under the seat.

As she had thought, they weren't in a stable building but the inn yard, as if the driver was expected to return and move on without changing horses. For now, there was no one around.

Warily, she opened the carriage door and jumped stiffly down. She was getting too old for such work. Closing the door behind her, she walked to the horses as if she had every right to be there and stroked their noses. Their breathing had calmed and they seemed contented enough.

Lawson untied the highwayman's horse from the back of the carriage, hoping no one would notice it too quickly as it ambled around the yard. Then, she walked around and climbed up onto the box. Few people knew she was a coachman's daughter and had secretly driven the vehicles of a Sussex squire when she was ten years old. Of course, her father had sat beside her, but she had learned from him and never forgot.

Gathering the reins, she touched the horses lightly with the whip. "Walk on," she told them, and guided them in a circle around the yard until they faced the gateway. She walked them through it, her heart in her mouth in case she met the highwayman coming the other way. Would she have the courage to ride him down? Or at least threaten to. Surely, he would get out of the way by instinct.

The matter wasn't tested. She drove the horses out of the yard and onto the road, unhindered, heading back the way she had come at a fast trot.

"THIS IS PLEASANT," Torridon said. "I feel like a contented farmer, out for a Sunday stroll with his wife and baby son."

They were walking along the road side by side in the pleasant spring sunshine, with Mark the under-coachman toiling after them. The air, scented with fresh grass and flowers, was redolent with birds' song.

Frances smiled, for it seemed she didn't mind being held up. "Well, it's partially true."

"Some landowners do work their own land, nowadays," Torridon said. "It's becoming almost fashionable."

"I think Daxton does. And I suspect Tamar will to some extent, if only for lack of other labor. Do you think you would be good at it?"

"I might. I've been learning over the last year and have some changes planned. I shall probably muck in, as it were." He hesitated. "It was Andrew, not me, who learned about the land. All I cared for was soldiering. I'll never be like him. But I can be my own earl."

"You *are* your own earl," she said warmly. Never before their fraught reunion at Braithwaite Castle had he admitted feeling out of his depth in his new role. In fact, he had hidden it so well that she had never guessed. She had been so involved in her own feelings that she hadn't given enough time to his.

His fingers threaded through hers. "I would rather be yours."

She flushed under his heated gaze. "I made that vow more than a year ago."

He bent his head and kissed her lips. Her heart leapt, though it was hardly the moment for passion, with Mark walking behind them, Lawson in danger, and Ariadne getting away with the rubies... and a coach and horses hurtling along the road toward them.

Torridon released her, drawing her to the side of the road and behind him. He gave Jamie into her arms and turned back to face the oncoming horses.

"Oh no," Frances said in dismay. "It isn't that wretched highwayman back again, is it?" She had the sudden fear that he would run them off the road, and was about to climb into the ditch to protect Jamie, when Torridon spoke in astonishment.

"It isn't any man. It's... it's *Lawson!*"

Frances peered around him. The horses—their own familiar carriage horses—were slowing. And guiding them to an expert halt was indeed Lawson.

"Lawson, you *angel!*" Frances exclaimed, while Torridon and Mark went to the horses. "We were praying you would escape without harm but it never entered my head you'd manage to steal back our horses and carriage! He didn't hurt you, did he?"

"Never knew I was there!" Lawson said with contempt. "He stopped in an inn yard where I doubt you could see the carriage from the road, and just wandered off. I waited while they watered the horses and then drove them back here to find you."

Grinning, Mark reached up to help her down from the box. "Well, what a hand you are, Miss Lawson, and no mistake. You'll be doing me out of a job next."

"Nonsense," Lawson said gruffly, though for the first time in Frances's company, she blushed. Turning to glare at Frances, she commanded, "Into the coach with you! His little lordship's been out in the sun too long."

"For once," Torridon said, opening the coach door, "you have precedence over all of us." And he handed Lawson into the carriage as though she were a great lady. Lawson seemed too stunned to protest, until she sat down inside and emitted a very un-Lawson-like giggle.

FRANCES HAD BEEN fifteen years old, Serena a year younger, and Gervaise all of nineteen summers when they had discovered the wonder of the ruined church. Of course, the grooms had already teased them that it was haunted, and they had first seen it rising out of a drifting mist, so it had been a wonderful place to make up stories and scare each other.

Coming upon it in adulthood during the late afternoon sunshine didn't quite have the same effect. It was merely a picturesque ruin. And, peering out of the carriage window, Frances could see no sign of anyone lurking among the broken walls.

"Perhaps we've missed them," she said, sitting back in disappointment. "Where would they go, next? To The Crown for tonight, then on to London in the morning…"

"Hmm." As the carriage halted, Torridon leaned over to inspect the ruins. "I certainly can't imagine her skulking behind broken walls for hours or sleeping under the stars. It doesn't look as if there is any of the roof left."

"There is, just at the back." Frances pointed toward the most substantial part of the ruin. "From there, you can see the way down to an undercroft. But the door is made of iron and locked fast. For safety, I suppose. The vicar at the new church—look, you can just make it out behind the trees—is quite proud of his ruin and looks after it."

Torridon's shoulder pressed against her back. His face was close to hers. Her whole body tingled with awareness. He reached past her, opening the door, and jumped down into the road.

"I think I'll just take a stroll over there and have a closer look. Mark, drive down the road a hundred yards or so, and see if you can't disguise the carriage a little in those trees at the bend. I won't be long."

With a quick smile at Frances, he closed the door, and walked off toward the ruin. The coach began to move, but Frances immediately knocked on the roof and it halted again.

"I'm going with him," Frances said, and gave the sleeping Jamie into Lawson's delighted arms. Then she, too, jumped down without the aid of steps, picked up her skirts, and hurried after her husband while the carriage lumbered off.

Although he must have heard her coming, he didn't look round. Instead, he waited until she fell into step beside him and simply took her hand. She smiled and they walked on together.

"You're not a very obedient wife, are you?" he said at last.

"No. But I saw you swipe the pistol from its pocket in the carriage. You think they're here, don't you?"

"I think they might be, but if our highway robbing friend is about, I don't want you here, too. We are just conducting a little reconnaissance."

Whatever the reason, there was pleasure in wandering among the ruins with him, a very different enjoyment to that of her childhood with Gervaise and Serena, but just as real. She said guiltily, "I probably shouldn't have left the castle so suddenly. I didn't mention Maria's problem to anyone else. With Serena gone, you don't suppose she'll do anything foolish, do you?"

"No," Torridon said. "Between you and me, she was trying to talk herself out of eloping with him this morning. I believe she would have, too. But I went with her in support, to give the young lieutenant his congé."

"You did?" Frances said, startled. "When?"

"While the rest of you were preventing Serena loading up the kitchen sink. And I'll tell you what, Frances, he's a paltry fellow, utterly undeserving of any female companion, let alone your sister."

"That bad?"

"Worse," Torridon said. "But his so-called friend seemed a good fellow. Bernard Muir? Heath had borrowed his curricle, but he came to talk them out of it."

Frances smiled. "I like Bernard. He's Gillie's brother."

"I know."

"How was Maria?" Frances asked with foreboding.

"Relieved mostly and a little sad. But I think she will get over it quickly."

"I suspect Serena's leaving had something to do with it all. We must make her feel more special."

"I agree."

Frances smiled at him, but he was gazing around the ruins.

"What happened to this place?" he asked.

"I don't believe anything *happened* to it except old age, and a landowner who wanted a grander church. Then his descendant became Viscount Overton and acquired more lucrative lands in the south. I don't think the family ever visit any more. Certainly, I've never met them up here. But I'm very grateful they left us a haunted ruin."

The sun ducked suddenly behind a bank of cloud, darkening the scene. A ghostly murmur seemed to whisper amongst the grass at her feet and a chill passed up her spine.

She halted mid-step, staring up at Torridon. "Did you hear that?"

He didn't answer. Gazing around him, he was obviously listening, too, as the echo of muffled voices drifted on the breeze and faded. He walked on. "I don't believe in ghosts. But I understand why the locals call it haunted."

"Serena swore she heard voices once. I thought she was making it up to scare us."

Torridon drew her on to the substantial part of the ruin, through the broken, arched doorway into a room with ivy growing out of the ceiling. "That will be your undercroft?" he observed, gesturing toward the iron door.

"Look through the keyhole," Frances advised. "You can see steep steps leading downward..." She broke off with a surge of excitement and lowered her voice. "Oh, do you think the sounds came from down there? There must be another way in."

Torridon, who had crouched to put his eye to the keyhole, rose to his feet, and pushed gently at the door. To Serena's astonishment, it swung silently open.

"There is a light shining from the foot of the stairs," he murmured in her ear. "Perhaps it's the vicar practicing black arts."

Laughter caught in the back of her throat.

"I wish you would wait here," he said, brushing his lips against her earlobe. She shivered. "If you won't, stay behind me."

In truth, since he immediately stepped through the doorway onto the first step, she could only remain behind him, for the winding stairs were too narrow to go side by side. Besides, there was no rail on the edge of the steps, so it seemed sensible to descend as close to the wall as possible.

As they did, the voices grew louder and more distinct. Many candles must have been lit to penetrate the darkness below, for there was enough light to guide their footsteps on the stairs.

A very echoey female voice drifted up to them. "It's freezing in here. And damp. I couldn't possibly have spent the night in such a place."

Frances frowned, for behind the distortion of the bare room be-low, was a distinct familiarity in that voice. She wasn't surprised.

"Then it's as well I found you more comfortable transport," a male voice responded. "If your ladyship could manage a short stroll."

"How did you achieve that?" the woman, who was surely Ariadne, asked with lazy amusement.

"I held up a carriage and—er—took it. I even got the inn to feed and water the horses. They'll be good and rested by the time we reach them. And we can travel by moonlight. How romantic is that?"

The highwayman! Without the ridiculous Scottish accent, of course. An elusive familiarity nagged at Frances. Did she not know that voice, too?

Ariadne gave a derisive laugh. "I suppose you will tell me you are responsible for the stars, too?"

As they rounded the next turn, Frances could see Ariadne and the highwayman, without his disguising hat and face-covering kerchief. They sat on a blanket in the middle of the huge, stone room. The rug was surrounded by a ring of candles, and between Ariadne and the highwayman laid a large heap of coins, jewels, and banknotes. Frances's own reticule lay open nearby, as though tossed aside when the meagre contents were emptied out.

They had not locked the door above, presumably because they were planning to leave soon and did not expect visitors. How had they got the key? Frances suspected there were several copies around. No doubt thieves and smugglers and vagrants had been using this place for decades, their drifting voices adding to the "haunted" rumors and serving to keep people away.

At the foot of the stairs, Torridon took the pistol from his pocket. Frances' heart beat faster, not so much with alarm as with the need to confront Ariadne with her perfidy. Especially when they drew nearer and her old friend changed position, revealing that she actually wore the rubies around her throat and dangling from her ears.

A quick, anxious scan of their surroundings showed Frances no sign of the highwayman's pistols. Nor could she see the overcoat he had stashed them in on their last meeting.

It was he who saw them first, turning his head as if at some faint sound. His eyes widened, but not as much as Frances's as she finally recognized the highwayman.

So, apparently, did Torridon. "Tom Marshall," he said in admiration. "Congratulations on your revival."

"Never dead, old boy," Tom Marshall drawled, while his wife jerked her head around in astonishment. "Just escaping a few too-pressing debts."

"Which you left your wife to pay for," Frances said indignantly, forgetting for a moment how angry she was with her supposed friend.

"Well," Tom said easily, never taking his eyes of Torridon, "people don't dun the beautiful widow quite so hard. It gave us a few months until my new trade could bring in a little of the readies. Not bearing a grudge, are you, old man?"

"About you pointing loaded pistols and my wife and child?" Torridon said in a voice that froze Frances's blood. "Oh yes, dead man, I *am* bearing a grudge."

"Oh, dear God in heaven, you imbecile!" Ariadne exclaimed, glaring at her husband. "Did you not recognize them?"

"Of course I did," Marshall said impatiently. "I've held up several people I recognize, as it happens. The whole point is rather that *they* don't recognize *me*. Going to shoot me, my lord?"

"Why not?" Torridon said carelessly. "Since you're dead already, it's really a free shot. For the moment, I'm holding it in reserve. My wife's rubies, ma'am, if you please."

As if she couldn't help it, Ariadne reached behind her neck, then dropped her hands again. "The clasp is too difficult. I can't manage it on my own."

Frances walked toward her.

"If you even look at my wife the wrong way," Torridon warned. "I'll shoot your husband."

"Go ahead," Ariadne said bitterly. "It will save me the trouble."

Marshall laughed. "Marital bliss, eh, Torridon?" he drawled.

Frances bent and found the necklace clasp.

"I'm sorry, Fran," Ariadne murmured with a surprising shade of anxiety in her voice. "You don't hate me for this, do you?"

Frances loosened the clasp and caught the heavy necklace. "I don't think we're on first name terms any more, *Mrs. Marshall*. The earrings, if you please."

"I wouldn't have stolen them if they were yours," Ariadne pleaded, obeying. "They were *his*. You kept telling me so."

"You knew how much they meant to me and why," Frances burst out, snatching the earrings from her erstwhile friend. "Even if you won the bet—and you did, in fact, for my husband recognized me before the ball—we had agreed on *one night*." She straightened, searching Ariadne's face. She wanted to be dignified, behave as coolly as Torridon, but it wasn't in her. This was betrayal. "I would have given you the money if you'd asked. I would have sold my own jewels to give you what you needed."

Ariadne laughed with an unexpected hint of bitterness. "Where would have been the fun in that? And we did have fun, did we not?"

Frances stepped back. "No. Because you manipulated me from the beginning, to make me hand over the rubies, to come here so that you could meet your supposedly dead husband at my expense."

"Are we counting a few shillings between us now, Fran? Is that what our friendship is worth in the end?"

Frances stared at her. "Apparently. You made it so."

Ariadne lifted her chin. "He's my husband."

And what of Sylvester Gaunt and all the other lovers? Frances wanted to hurl the accusation, especially in front of Tom Marshall, to wound and destroy. But love came in many forms, and it seemed, even now, she would not risk Ariadne's. If such it was.

"Your rubies were our retirement," Tom said casually. "I had a buyer lined up in America and we were going to take ship from Liverpool. Until I heard Ariadne had stopped here and I rode up to join her."

Keeping the pistol pointed at Tom, Torridon bent and picked up

Frances's reticule. She took it from him without a word and dropped the rubies inside it.

"The game is over," Torridon said flatly. "If it ever was one, it stopped being so as soon as you threatened my family. You may keep the money—no one will ever be able to sort out now how much came from whom. But I shall take the rest to a magistrate and the law will be on your heels. You'd better take ship quickly."

Keeping the pistol level, Torridon moved to the side, away from the stolen treasure spread over the rug. "Frances, be so good as to retrieve the… er… plunder."

As she moved, she finally saw the highwayman's coat. Tom was sitting on it.

"Have a heart," Marshall protested. "How can we live lawfully in America if you take away our means?"

"Lawfully?" Frances said indignantly, snatching up necklaces and snuffboxes and stuffing them into her reticule. "You'd be living on the sale of stolen goods!"

"They're gewgaws," Marshall said. "Easily replaceable baubles belonging to people who already have too much."

"By which you mean, *more than you*," Frances retorted. There was no more space in her reticule, so she spread out a silk shawl and bundled the other items onto it. "And you don't know that. You have no idea what these *gewgaws* meant to their owners, what damage you might have caused. Why do you imagine the rest of the world owes you, when you've never worked at anything in your life?"

Marshall's eyes seemed to snap suddenly and he leaned forward. "I beg to differ," he drawled. "I worked damned hard at being a highwayman. And I was good at it."

There was an instant when she looked into his face and knew. But it was already too late. His right hand was lost in the coat beneath him. Torridon had seen the movement and hurled himself forward.

Why doesn't he shoot? Even as the thought flitted through her brain, she knew the answer. Torridon was afraid he was aiming at her, and trying to throw himself between Frances and Marshall's pistol.

A sharp explosion rent the air an instant before Torridon landed on top of Marshall. Frances even glimpsed the smoking, singed hole in the coat. She stumbled forward, unsure what she could do, just determined to try. Ariadne caught her hand as three pistols skidded across the floor in rapid succession, and the heaving mass of male limbs resolved into two men once more.

Torridon heaved Marshall to his feet, forcing one arm up his back so ungently that the highwayman squawked.

Frances wrenched her hand free of Ariadne's and hurried on trembling legs to pick up her husband's pistol and whichever of Marshall's was still loaded. Her hands shook, but she found the heavier pistol and rose with it held gingerly in her left hand pointing downward.

Only then, when she turned to face the others, did she see the scarlet blood dripping over her husband's snowy white cuff and onto the floor. The world tilted in terror.

"Actually, you weren't good at it," Torridon said, not even out of breath as he reverted to the previous conversation as if nothing had happened.

"Good at what?" Marshall panted furiously.

"Being a highwayman. A lady's maid drove the carriage back to us and we followed you here."

Marshall scowled, twisting round to stare at him. And then he laughed.

"You're bleeding!" Ariadne exclaimed, starting toward Torridon. "Tom, you imbecile, you shot him!" Her skin was unnaturally white in the flickering candlelight as she swept up to him.

"I'm fine," Torridon said impatiently. "It's a scratch with barely any blood. His aim is shocking—he only hit me at all by accident."

"You moved," Marshall accused, but his gaze remained on his wife. A funny little smile played about his lips. "I see. So that's the lie of the land."

"Don't be a bigger fool than you already are," Ariadne retorted. For an instant, her eyes met Torridon's, and an unlikely suspicion sprang into Frances's head. Then Ariadne swung around to her. "Let us go," she said abruptly. "You have your rubies, and most of what we would have used to begin a new life in America. We'll vanish without scandal. You don't want your names dragged into this sordid affair, which they will be if you bring the law into it."

Frances met the gaze of her old friend, her stomach twisting with loss and possibly the ultimate betrayal.

"For auld lang syne," Ariadne said.

Frances's lips twisted. "For auld lang syne." She glanced at Torridon, anxious to get him away, to see to his wound and get him to a doctor. "Shall we go?"

Torridon shoved Marshall away from him so that he stumbled and righted himself, rubbing his twisted arm. By then, Torridon had retrieved both pistols from Frances. "Bring the fired one, too. I wouldn't put it past him to reload it and shoot us in the back."

Frances obeyed, trying to force her mind to the task rather than to the painful speculation caused by that look in Ariadne's eyes when she'd seen Torridon bleeding. *So that's the lie of the land...* here was another slow, gaping wound, a betrayal far worse than that of a friend.

But she couldn't allow such suspicion, not now. They had to get out of there safely. She had to see to Torridon's injury and feed Jamie.

Laughter caught in her throat at the bizarre turn this day had taken. And yet the basics remained just as important.

Carrying her heavy reticule, Frances swept up the silk shawl and tied it into a bundle containing the rest of the stolen treasures. Then, she walked across the vaulted chamber to the stairs, occasionally looking back to make sure Torridon didn't stumble over something behind him, for he walked backward, the pistols still pointed at Tom Marshall.

As they began to climb the stairs, Ariadne said, "Frannie."

And in spite of herself, she glanced back over her shoulder.

Ariadne smiled. "We *did* have fun, didn't we?"

Frances could have ignored the question or made some crushing denial. One hovered on her tongue. But her throat ached. She couldn't lie and didn't want to.

"We did," she whispered. "I wish you luck, Ari." She hurried up the stairs and through the door into the brightness of daylight above.

Torridon closed the door with a slam, added two of the pistols to her bundle, and took it from her. "Hurry," he said grimly. "I don't trust either of them."

But as they strode through the ruins, she could hear the less-than-ghostly voices shouting at each other in furious argument. Torridon's lips curled and he glanced at Frances, inviting her to share the sardonic joke.

"I think we're safe," she said with a breath of laughter that hurt.

Chapter Sixteen

MARK HAD ALREADY turned the carriage so that it waited perpendicular to the road and was ready to go in either direction. Frances directed him to take the back roads home to Blackhaven, mainly so that they would be nowhere near Whalen if and when the Marshalls boarded a ship there.

But her biggest concern was Torridon's wound. And as soon as he had sat down beside her, and she'd acknowledged Jamie who was being dandled on Lawson's knee, she began unbuttoning her husband's coat.

"Frances," he protested.

"If you can take it off yourself, do so," she returned briskly. "And tear the sleeve of your shirt if need be so that we can see your wound."

"Oh, no!" Lawson exclaimed. "Did that devil shoot his lordship?"

"His lordship insists he scratched him," Frances replied, kneeling on the bumping coach floor to retrieve the medicine box that was kept beneath the seat. "And the devil in question is none other than Tom Marshall. They're on their way to America."

There was a pause. Frances was sure the maid's jaw had dropped, but her focus was all on Torridon's bared arm. With a flask of water and clean cloth, she wiped the blood away from the wound. He bore her ministrations without flinching, his gaze steady on her face.

The ball had gouged a lump of flesh from his upper arm, but to her inexperienced eye, had caused more damage to his coat, which had two singed holes in it.

"It's only a graze," Torridon said soothingly. "The ball just nicked me by accident. It will heal in no time. Let me—"

She batted his hand away and placed a dressing over the wound, which was still sluggishly bleeding. Then she wound a bandage around it to keep it in place. "This will do until the doctor sees it," she said gruffly. Feeling his gaze still burning her face, she looked up at him and swallowed. "It might not be serious," she said, low, "but it must hurt horrendously. How did you fight him like that?"

His lips quirked. "I'm a soldier. Or at least, I was. I've fought with worse. Most of us did."

"Then she really did abandon me," Lawson said. If she saw that Frances poured the rest of the water over her hands and dried them on her gown, she ignored the crime. Clearly, she was distressed.

"Only for her husband," Frances said. It seemed the kindest thing to say.

"I *knew* I had heard his voice before," Lawson said. "He was right, though. That ridiculously broad Scots accent did disguise him. It just never entered my head..."

"Well, it wouldn't," Torridon observed. "The man was supposed to be dead."

"I should have known when she didn't grieve," Lawson said thoughtfully. "Oh, I know she can be coldhearted and she's always been fond of other gentlemen, but I could have sworn there was more affection for him. And yet, she never wept. Not even in private."

Torridon grunted. "Well, I hope they'll both be very happy together. Somewhere well away from these shores."

Frances kicked the medicine box back under the seat and regarded him surreptitiously. There was too much intensity in his abrupt voice. He was keeping something from her. Something else. Just when they had reached a new understanding, a reconciliation that promised even greater happiness than before, was she to discover at the last that he had been her friend's lover?

When?

Jealousy and betrayal pierced her like a dagger, twisting through her stomach to her heart. Her hand crept to her breast as though she could soothe it. Jamie began to make discontented noises, so she reached for him instead.

"I'm starving, too," Torridon remarked. "Do you know we've eaten nothing all day?"

They stopped at a village inn that was little more than a public house, and Torridon acquired some small beer, bread and pies, paying with a few coins that had fortunately got caught up in the stolen jewelry retrieved from the Marshalls. Not that it would have really mattered. Frances's face was known in the area and would always have ensured them credit.

Since it was growing late, they ate while travelling. Lawson's instinctive disapproval at such informality quickly thawed into something akin to awe. Although, a trace of misery returned to her voice when she realized they would not return to Blackhaven via Whalen.

"May I beg for transport to Whalen in time for the stagecoach tomorrow?" she asked. "I can pay, for I still have the money your ladyship gave me at the hotel so—"

"Of course you may," Torridon interrupted. "And there will be no payment. We already owe you more than that. You may return to London whenever you wish, at our expense. However, if you prefer it, there is a place for you in our household."

"There is," Frances agreed, touched because she had not even needed to ask him.

Lawson flushed pink with pleasure, but Frances wasn't yet up to planning her precise position with them. She already had an abigail, although not at Blackhaven. In truth, as her fear for Torridon's safety relaxed, her suspicion grew more and more intense, robbing her of what should have been pleasure in this homecoming. The easy closeness of their earlier journey had quite gone. She kept to her own end of the seat with Jamie, avoiding her husband's touch and even his gaze.

Torridon, however, did not notice. Or at least, she thought he didn't. He gazed out of the window at the Black Fort, from which only a couple of months ago, a French prisoner had escaped. She wanted to mention it to him, a safe yet intriguing topic of conversation that, according to Serena, involved one of Tamar's sisters. But his stare was fixed on the window and the hunch of his shoulder seemed somehow repelling. He was deep in thought, and in truth, so was she. And so, she let the moment pass and the carriage trundled on. They would be back at the castle soon, probably just as dusk fell.

Abruptly, Torridon reached up and rapped on the roof and the coach slowed to a halt. Torridon took the sleeping baby from Frances, placing him instead in Lawson's delighted arms.

"I feel the need to stretch my legs, so her ladyship and I shall walk the rest of the way. If you're at the castle before us, Mark will see you to the servants' hall and make sure you're looked after until we arrive." He opened the door and alighted, then let down the steps and peremptorily held out his hand to Frances.

She stared at him, bewildered and ready to refuse as much from perversity as from fear of hearing what he wanted to say in private. But she had never been a coward.

"Thank you, Lawson," she said, and stepped down onto the side of the road.

Mark, who clearly thought them mad for giving up the comfort of the carriage at this stage, merely saluted them with his whip and drove on.

Torridon offered her his arm and led her off the road completely. "We can go across country from here, can we not?"

"Yes. It's quicker. We'll probably arrive at the same time as the carriage going via the road. But we'll need a lantern if we don't hurry."

There was a little-used track through the woods that Frances found easily enough. Only then did she ask, "Do you really need to stretch your legs, or have you something private to say?"

"I thought you had something to discuss," Torridon replied. "We agreed we should have no more secrets—they only lead to misunderstandings. So, ask me what you want to know."

Is Ariadne your mistress? Was she ever your mistress? She tightened her grip on his sleeve, appalled by the impossibility of asking such questions. They went against her own pride as much as against her training as a lady never to "notice" her husband's straying, or even to acknowledge the existence of such women.

"You are silent," he said quietly. "And yet I know there is something bothering you."

"I'm not sure I want to know the answer," she confessed. "In time, I could live happily in ignorance."

He smiled, and her heart leapt at the tenderness in his eyes. "No, you couldn't, Frances. It isn't in your nature."

She bit her lower lip, working around the subject. Perhaps she would not need to ask. "Did you know Ariadne before you met me?"

He considered. "No, I believe I encountered you both for the first time when I came to London the season before last."

That didn't help her. In fact, it made things worse, for she could have forgiven any intimacy before he had met her, put any silence on the subject down to his desire not to hurt her rather to deception. Alan was not a deceitful man. If she knew anything about him, it was that.

"Did you... like her?" Frances managed.

"No," he said flatly. "At first, I barely noticed her, and once I did, my dislike only grew with acquaintance. I made little secret of the fact I did not care for your friendship with her."

She gazed into the trees. The silence seemed to shroud her like some heavy garment, weighing her down. Even the birds had stopped singing.

Torridon swore below his breath and stopped, swinging her round to face him and seizing her by both shoulders. "Let me make it easy for you. I was not used to London manners. I didn't even realize she was pursuing me until after you and I were engaged. Then, after some ball or other, when I was walking home, she stopped her carriage and invited me to her home."

Frances closed her eyes. *It doesn't matter. It is past. It doesn't matter.* In time, it would not hurt.

"Marshall was away somewhere," Torridon continued relentlessly, "although no one had yet called him dead. I declined and walked on."

Her eyes flew open of their own accord, staring into his.

His lips quirked. "That is the extent of any intimacy between us. If you sense some… feeling from her toward me, it is not returned, nor ever was. I expect it is largely pique because I am the only man ever to resist her. And for me, it was easy, because my heart, my head, my life was full only of you. Frances—"

With a sob, she hurled herself against him and reached for his mouth.

His kiss was hard, almost savage, and she flung her arms up around his neck in abandon. Every fiber of her being responded to his passion as he crushed her to him and plundered her open, willing mouth. Slowly, gradually, the kiss gentled, yet became more blatantly sensual, arousing. His hardness pressed against her, thrilling her.

He groaned into her mouth. "My sweet, my love," he whispered. "You will undo me…"

A gurgle of excited laughter rose to her lips. "Here?"

He laughed softly and kissed her again. His arms, his whole body shook as he fought to control his passion and won. His hold loosened enough to let her breathe easily. "I have waited so long for this," he whispered against her lips. "So long… when I finally get you home, all to myself, there will be no more waiting. *Ever.*"

Her heart thundered in her ears. It was all she could hear, apart from her own panting breath and his.

"Why wait?" she whispered. "There is no one here nor likely to be at this time. We are alone and it is not cold." She closed her mouth over his again. He kissed her back as though he couldn't help it, but slowly, gently, however reluctantly, he was putting her from him, pushing her away. Again.

She tore herself free. "What is *wrong* with me?" she demanded, swiping her hand across her eyes.

"Wrong with you?" he repeated in clear astonishment. "Nothing. Absolutely nothing."

She drew in a shuddering breath and would have walked on along the path, except he stood in her way, holding her once more by the shoulders, staring down into her face.

"Frances, what is it?" he asked, helplessly.

She closed her eyes, as if that would somehow make things easier to say. "There is passion in you," she whispered. "I feel it. Deep, intense, urgent, and yet… it is not for me, is it? If you love me, it is not… like that."

His grip tightened. When she forced her eyes open, he stared down into them as though straight into her soul.

"God help me, I love you every way there is," he said unsteadily. "But I am a large man with large desires, and I would die rather than hurt a hair on your head."

She reached up and took his face between her hands, loving the roughness of his jaw, the soft texture of his lips under her thumbs. "I am not porcelain, Alan. I won't break. Give in. Give in to what you want of me because I want it, too."

There was a moment when she wondered if she had lost again, and then with a groan, he seized her mouth in his and she gasped with joy at his abandon. She clung to his neck, tugging the soft hair at his nape. "Here?" he whispered between kisses. "Here and now? Truly?"

"Truly," she said fervently and reached for his mouth again. But he spun her around so fast that she grasped onto a tree trunk for support. Her cloak fell to the ground as his lips seized her nape, kissing and nibbling while his fingers tugged at the laces of her gown and chemise. She gasped as they fell around her feet and his arms closed around her naked body, protecting her from the chilly air, dragging her back against him. His avid hands, his lips, were everywhere, caressing her greedily from breast to thigh, and then inward to the flaring, desperate heat of her lust.

She cried out at his touch, twisting her head to see his stormy face, his clouded eyes burning with passion. She had aroused the devil in him at last, and she was almost frightened. Almost.

He kissed her mouth. "Say you want this," he said fiercely. "Say you want me."

"I want you," she sobbed, and he entered her in one smooth thrust.

From there, it was quick and wild and the most exciting thing she had ever known. There only his swift, demanding body, his worshiping hands and lips, the scrape of the tree bark against her breasts. Inside and out she rose to crashing, consuming bliss. And more even than that, his glorious, uninhibited shout of completion made her weep with joy. Now, at last, he was hers.

As THE CARRIAGE drew to the top of the drive, the front door of the castle opened and a dignified, middle-aged butler stepped out. Lawson opened the carriage door herself as servants ran to the horses' heads and a footman let down the steps for her. She stepped out with the baby in her arms, hoping somewhat nervously that Lord and Lady Torridon would not be long.

"Where are they?" the footman demanded urgently. "Where is Lady Frances?"

"She's walking the rest of the way with her husband," Lawson replied. "They'll be here directly. She instructed me to bring his little lordship straight here."

"It's true enough," Mark said. "This here is Lawson, who serves Lady Frances. Take her inside, will you? And maybe best inform her *young* ladyship…"

But there was no time to pick and choose. The butler was summoning them to the front entrance, and as soon as Lawson stepped over the door, she stopped dead, confronted by a row of strangers. Two formidable middle-aged ladies, a younger one, and a tall, frowning gentleman. The butler and Mrs. Gaskell—the housekeeper whom she had met before while carrying Lady Torridon's message to the mysterious foreign gentleman—advanced purposefully upon her.

But one of the older matrons thrust herself suddenly forward, all but charging at Lawson. "Give the child to me at once. I am Lady

Torridon!"

Lawson, who had instinctively shielded Jamie from the onslaught, reluctantly let the icy lady take him from her.

The Dowager Lady Torridon swung away from her in triumph, Jamie held like a trophy in her arms. "There, my poor child, you are safe now," she announced. Then adjusting her grip, she pointed with loathing at Lawson. "Hold that woman and send for the magistrate!"

THEY LAY ON the soft, spongy earth at the foot of the tree. Torridon wrapped her in his arms and her cloak and hugged her close. He still couldn't quite believe what he had just done to his sweet, delicate wife. But then, he hadn't so much done it *to* her as *with* her. He could doubt neither her full cooperation nor her pleasure. He smiled into her shoulder and kissed it, and she slipped her arms around him, purring like a cat.

"You," he murmured, "are a very wicked wife."

"I am an obedient wife," she said contentedly. "Submitting to my husband's desires."

He kissed her. "I think I was afraid that was all you would do, if I was anything other than gentle and…"

"Polite," she interjected.

"I was never merely polite," he disputed, kissing the corner of her mouth. "And I always brought you pleasure."

She slid her hand down his back to his hip, slipping under his shirt and his half-unbuttoned pantaloons. "You did. But I love your spontaneity even more."

He kissed her for a long time and almost took her again. But the ground was damp and dusk was falling fast. And he would have her again tonight. All night…

His body thrumming with fresh anticipation, he reached for her clothes and dressed her, with many kisses before covering each favorite part of her.

"I've torn your gown," he noticed, fastening it behind her as best he could. "I will have to be your maid for tonight."

"I'll like that," she said huskily.

God, he loved her. All of her, and there were always new facets to discover, like this delicious new sensuality he would be hard-pushed to leave alone. He couldn't remember ever being so aroused or so sweetly, massively satisfied.

He righted his own clothes and drew them both to their feet, before halfheartedly brushing crushed grass and old leaves from them. Then he took her in his arms and kissed her thoroughly, just because he wanted to. She looked so adorable and wanton.

"You are wonderful," he whispered. "I will so enjoy bringing you to new pleasures, new heights."

She smiled as he combed out her hair with his fingers and crouched to retrieve all her fallen pins. She seemed surprised when he re-pinned her hair very neatly.

"You have done this too often before," she said, with mock severity, taking his hand as they walked back onto the path.

"I've been no saint," he confessed. "I enjoy women. But there was never anyone like you."

She leaned her head against his shoulder for a moment. "Nor you. I was so thrilled—and relieved—when my mother regarded you as a serious and suitable suitor."

"What would you have done if she hadn't?"

"I don't know. Pined, probably, most romantically."

"Would you have run away with me?"

"If you'd asked."

He gazed down at her. "Truly? That was my alternative plan."

She laughed. "Well, it would have been fun, but at least this way, we don't have to quarrel with our families and be ostracized."

They walked on in companionable silence, enfolded in the gathering dusk, as if they were the only two people in the world, with only the few creatures scuttling in the undergrowth for company. It was only for a few more minutes, of course, but in those minutes, he didn't think he had ever been so completely, utterly happy.

As they emerged from the trees, looking across at the castle, he said, "What do you want to do? Where would you like to go when we leave here?"

"Everywhere," she said promptly. "Anywhere. Wouldn't it be fun to travel, once this wretched war ends?"

"It's more or less ended now. We could go for a month in the summer, probably."

"And I would like to go to Tamar Abbey, maybe in the autumn?"

"Why not, if they'll have us? And London?"

"If you wish."

"I do have to spend some time in Torridon."

She blinked. "Of course you do." She peered up at him. "You are thinking I am unhappy there," she said. "But I'm not. I like the country and the people. I was only unhappy without *you*. And other company," she admitted, "but chiefly, you."

His fingers tightened on hers before he drew her hand into his arm in a more decorous pose for approaching the castle. "I'm sorry. I was trying to be a good and considerate husband. And almost ended by not being a husband at all."

"We have to talk to each other," she said seriously. "Without pride or fear of any kind."

He couldn't take his eyes off her face. "I love you," he said quietly. "More than life itself."

Even in the dim light that was left, he could see the sparkle of unshed tears brimming in her eyes. For an instant, he was appalled to have made her cry. But she pressed her cheek to his arm.

"I never thought you would say that to me," she whispered. "And mean it."

"I could never have said it and not meant it."

"Neither could I. But then, I have only ever loved you."

Regardless of any watching eyes, he kissed her. She cooperated so charmingly that he was tempted to walk back into the woods. But they had left Jamie with Lawson, and it was dinner time.

Paton himself opened the front door to them, a warning frown on his face that Torridon could not account for. He cast the butler a quizzical glance. And then, as they walked into the house, the next person he saw was his mother with Jamie in her arms.

Chapter Seventeen

FRANCES HALTED IN sheer shock. Lady Torridon was the last person in the world she wanted to see. All the joy of her recent encounter with Alan and the new closeness between them was too new and wonderful to be subjected to her domineering mother-in-law quite so soon.

Lady Torridon stood at the foot of the stairs, as though she had witnessed their approach from an upper window and had come down to be the first to greet them. Or at least berate them, for she didn't look remotely pleased to see them. Her eyes flashed with fury across the entrance hall. Her lips were pinched in disapproval.

"Mother," Torridon said blankly. "What in the world are you doing here?"

"Looking for you," she snapped.

And as if he felt her anger, Jamie began to cry, and Frances's paralysis broke. She hurried across the hall, uttering a civil greeting to her mother-in-law, though her attention was all on Jamie.

She reached for him, smiling. "What an ill-mannered, noisy boy you are. What will your grandmother think of you?"

But Lady Torridon spun away, snatching the baby clear of her. "You should be more concerned what I think of *you*. You stole him away from his home, galivanting God knows where with that woman, and finally abandoned him with some stranger! Well, I have called for the magistrate to deal with *her*."

"Called for the…" With an effort, Frances bit back her outrage. "Lawson is not a stranger and is perfectly capable of looking after

Jamie for half an hour," she said, trying to remain calm although her hackles had risen. More than that, an instinctive panic rose fast, along with the need to see to her crying child. "Give him to me, please. He is hungry."

"I have brought a suitable wet nurse with me to care for such needs," Lady Torridon said contemptuously. "You will never again have the care of the future Earl of Torridon."

All Frances's training as a lady fought with her instincts, which told her to slap the countess and snatch back her son. She would not have such malevolence near him. But neither would she frighten Jamie with such violence or a physical tug of war that could end in hurting him.

So, as calmly as she could, she said, "Lady Torridon, you will please pass my son to me. You have no reason and less right to behave like this. We can discuss your concerns later, once Jamie is fed and content."

She held out her arms, but again Lady Torridon held him away from her. "You," she commanded, and Frances glanced at the footman being addressed.

Harry, his expression appalled rather than wooden-faced as normal, bowed to the countess, though hostility radiated from every inch of him.

"Fetch Meg Campbell to me," Lady Torridon commanded.

Harry looked deliberately at Frances, whom he had known most of his life and hers. "My lady?"

"I've no idea who Meg Campbell is," Frances said. "By all means bring her to Lady Torridon. Once she is relieved of the burden of my son."

"You are unfit!" Lady Torridon cried, no longer even troubling to lower her voice. Even Torridon, who was clearly being brought up to the moment by Paton with events at the castle, heard that, for his impetuous footsteps tore across the parquet floor behind Frances.

"What's more," Lady Torridon hissed. "I have begun legal proceedings to have you…"

"Mother," Torridon's voice thundered, causing both Frances and her mother-in-law to jump. Even Jamie stopped crying in surprise, although he began again almost immediately. "When you have handed my distressed son to his mother, be so good as to come upstairs."

"I have no intention—" Lady Torridon broke off.

Frances didn't blame her. She had never seen such a look of implacable fury on Alan's face. It was akin to that with which he had accused Tom Marshall of threatening her and Jamie, and yet very different, too. For he had expected better of his mother.

The dowager wanted to refuse. She had come ready and able for a fight, though not with her son. Clearly, she had never expected to be treated like one of his old, insubordinate soldiers. She swallowed audibly.

Frances took Jamie from her reluctant arms and cuddled him close, sailing up the stairs in front of her mother-in-law, murmuring soothing, nonsense words of love. Jamie quieted slowly, clearly still upset.

On the landing, she encountered Gervaise, who had no doubt been summoned by the servants to deal with the situation. "Is everything well?" he asked, taking in the scene at a glance.

"It is now," she assured him. "I'll just take him into the small drawing room, if it is quiet, and feed him there. It is the quickest way to calm him."

"Of course... do you need Eleanor?"

"No, though I shall always be glad of her company. Oh, Gervaise, could you look after Lawson, the maid who brought Jamie? Lady Torridon summoned Mr. Winslow—"

"I, however, did not," Braithwaite said flatly. "Mrs. Gaskell and Mark vouched for Lawson as someone of yours. And frankly, I could not see why some evil child stealer would bring the baby here to the castle! She's eating dinner in the servants' hall."

Frances smiled gratefully and hurried along the gallery to the smaller drawing room. She still trembled with anger, though she did her best to be calm for Jamie's sake.

Behind her, her husband said, "My apologies, Braithwaite. We seem to have brought a vulgar misunderstanding under your roof. It will be over directly."

"I look forward to seeing my sister after that." It was Gervaise's civil warning, which warmed France's heart. Even though there was no need, for her husband was defending her.

Throwing off her cloak, she took a comfortable armchair by the fire. Since Torridon had so impetuously torn the fastenings of her gown and chemise, it was easy to pull both garments downward and put Jamie to her breast.

Torridon filled the open doorway. "May my mother and I join you, or would you rather wait until later to have this discussion?"

"Now is acceptable, but if there are raised voices—"

"There will be no raised voices," Torridon assured her, standing aside for his mother to enter.

Frances wondered if this was deliberate, if he wanted his mother to see her feeding her son, to show her that whatever story she had convinced herself of was utterly false. Frances wasn't even sure it mattered. Lady Torridon wanted control and she didn't like Frances. She never had.

Alan closed the door and civilly conducted his mother to the chair on the other side of the fireplace to Frances. Lady Torridon, scandalized, looked away from the contentedly feeding baby.

"You should do that in the privacy of your bedchamber," she uttered.

"Normally, I do," Frances said evenly. "But we appear to have a crisis, and this is the nearest comfortable room."

"Anyone could come in."

"Nobody will, Mother," Torridon said impatiently. "Allow us both some sense."

"Sense!" his mother exclaimed. "When she bolts without a word and vanishes without trace for days on end? And is next seen in the company of that Marshall woman who, I take leave to tell you, is—"

"There is no need to tell us anything about Ariadne Marshall,"

Torridon interrupted. "We already know a great deal more than you do."

"That may be. I suppose you flew after her to get your son back. Then let us take him and be gone. This... *baggage* is no longer welcome at Torridon."

Frances blinked. If this conversation had occurred even last night, it might have given her a moment of fright. As it was, she had always found the insult "baggage" to be exquisitely humorous. Her giggle broke the ominous silence.

"You will apologize to my wife, Mother," Torridon said coldly. "And let me make it plain, since your own manners clearly don't, that you will never address her in such terms again. She is deserving of your respect, if not your love, and you will most certainly accord her the former."

"Respect is earned," Lady Torridon snapped.

"Oh, I think she has earned it by putting up with both of us with such grace for the last year. Don't you?"

Lady Torridon glanced up at him and was held in the cold fury of his stare. "She has ensnared you all over again with her pretty face and her insinuating ways. Can you not see she is unworthy—"

"I see all too clearly," he broke in. "And the unworthiness is not Frances's. Mother, let me be plain. There can be no legal proceedings concerning my son without me. Therefore, there will be none, ever. The whole idea is ludicrous. I will not have this nonsense. *Any* of this nonsense. Do you understand me? I will not have it. Frances is my wife, the mother of my son, the Countess of Torridon, and you will *not* undermine her, with me or anyone else."

"Fine. Then I shall move back to Drummany and leave you to cope—"

"You will most certainly do so and as quickly as possible," Torridon interrupted the threat with insulting speed. "Whether or not you are invited to visit again will be entirely in the hands of my wife."

It was brutal. There had been many times, in Torridon, when Frances had dreamed of him dismissing his mother in just such terms.

Now that he had, she knew suddenly that she could deal with her mother-in-law in her own home or anywhere else. She looked at Torridon and his lip quirked in understanding.

"Mother," he said, more gently. "Can you not see that between us, you and I made her so miserable that she had no choice but to bolt, as you put it? I have understood at last and apologized and I believe, if you think about it, you will, too. Frances, why don't we go upstairs and change for dinner? Now that he is calmer, you can finish feeding his lordship there."

"I believe I won't disturb him," Frances said, determined not to leave her mother-in-law in possession of the field. "But you go up. I shouldn't be long, now."

He glanced at her doubtfully, but when she nodded, he merely bowed with good grace and went out. There was silence in the room, apart from small baby noises.

Lady Torridon said stiffly, "He may be fooled. But you and I understand each other."

Frances regarded her. "Actually, I don't understand you and never have. I am willing to try but I will not tolerate hostility."

Lady Torridon goggled. "Tolerate?" she spluttered. "Hostility?"

"Just so," Frances said kindly. "Shall I ring for a glass of water?"

"Thank you, I am quite well!"

The door opened and Eleanor came in. There was nothing shy about the young countess now as she came to join them and sat on a stool by Frances's knee. She kept the conversation lively and civil, and in the end, it was Lady Torridon who stood first to go.

"Your brother is so lucky in his choice of bride," she said to Frances by way of a parting shot. "Such a prettily-behaved young lady."

As the door closed behind her, Eleanor's face broke into a mischievous grin. "If only she knew I was brought up by gypsies."

Frances laughed until she cried.

"DUELING?" DR. LAMPTON said with undisguised contempt as he inspected Torridon's wound. Mark had summoned him from Black-haven on his return to the castle, and Torridon now sat on the bed with his bandage and the bloody dressing beside him.

"No," Torridon said mildly. "A difference of opinion with a highwayman."

Dr. Lampton glanced at him with raised brows. "And the highwayman's condition?"

"Chastened," said Torridon. "And fleeing the country."

A flicker of amusement lit the doctor's eyes for a moment before they returned to the wound. He reached for his bag. "I think it will heal by itself. This will help." He took out a jar of muddy ointment and scooped some out on his finger.

Torridon regarded it with disfavor. "You didn't get that from a filthy old crone who lives in a cave, did you?"

"No." Dr. Lampton slathered it over the wound with surprising gentleness for such an apparently rough and sardonic individual. "From a pirate, actually. Don't be a baby."

Stunned into amused silence by this disrespect, Torridon let him anoint and bandage his arm.

"Do you need some laudanum for the pain?" Dr. Lampton asked.

Torridon shook his head.

"Change the dressing regularly," Lampton instructed. "And keep the wound scrupulously clean. If you see any signs of corruption, if it becomes even slightly hot or puffy around the edges, send for me again."

"I will. Thank you."

Lampton grunted and tossed the jar back into his bag. The bedchamber door opened and Frances walked in with Jamie.

"Ah, you must be Dr. Lampton," she said in her friendly way, offering her one free hand. "I have heard much about you."

"And you must be Lady Frances. Lady Torridon," he corrected himself, shaking her hand briefly. "I have heard much about you, too." His sharp eyes scanned Frances's face and dropped to Jamie. "You both look well," he offered, nodded curtly and walked out.

"Strange fellow," Torridon remarked.

"He's certainly not overwhelmed by rank," Frances said. "Apparently, he told Dax off for dueling. I suppose it was time somebody did. Serena told me he lost his wife and unborn child last year, so we must allow him a little shortness of temper. What did he say about your arm?"

"That it would heal by itself. What did my mother say to you?"

"That she wished I was Eleanor instead," Frances said, her eyes laughing.

Torridon pulled her down beside him and grinned back at his son. "You are very good-natured about her."

"I wasn't," Frances admitted. "But now that I am so happy, I find I can tolerate her. You don't have to send her away."

"It's time," Torridon said. "Long past time. For all our sakes. Put Jamie down and I'll help you change for dinner."

AFTERWARD, TORRIDON DESCRIBED that dinner at Braithwaite Castle as the Battle of the Dowagers. Both matriarchs tried to out-do each other with stories demonstrating the excellence of their sons, until both Braithwaite and Torridon were thoroughly embarrassed. The girls, allowed to join the grownups at Frances's persuasion, sniggered uncontrollably at their brother's discomfort. Even Maria hid a smile.

"I don't recognize him either," Frances assured them in low tones.

"What about Torridon?" Helen asked.

"No, but then I wasn't acquainted with him until little more than a year ago."

In the end, Lady Torridon won that battle by introducing the subject of her late first born to the conversation. No one with any feeling could try to trump his perfection—although Torridon cast his mother an ironic look that told Frances he didn't recognize his brother in this paragon either.

They moved on to sons-in-law—in which the honors were general-
ly considered to be even, since one of Lady Braithwaite's sons-in-law
was Torridon. The girls seemed likely to collapse under the table with
suppressed laughter.

The dowager Lady Braithwaite, somewhat slyly since she, like the
rest of the castle, must have been aware of the scene in the hall,
brought up daughters-in-law, praising Eleanor until that poor lady was
quite pink with embarrassment. And there they left it, since clearly
Lady Torridon had nothing good to say about Frances.

Instead, she turned suddenly to Frances as if the thought had just
occurred to her. "Where is my grandson?"

Frances smiled. "With Lawson, ma'am. In our bedchamber, where
he sleeps. Eleanor, would you mind very much if we stayed another
few days? Just until Mama and the girls go south, and then we shall
return to Torridon."

"I shall be glad of it," Eleanor said at once. "We're not going to
London for a fortnight." She turned to Lady Torridon. "And what of
yourself, ma'am? Do you care to stay for a little?"

"You are too kind to an uninvited guest," Lady Torridon said graciously. "But I have much to do at Torridon. I must leave in the
morning."

"My mother has been helping us there for some time," Torridon
remarked. "But she has decided it's time to return to her own
establishment."

"Indeed," the dowager said frostily.

By the time the ladies moved to the drawing room, the dowagers
had moved onto the subject of daughters. Unable to bear it, Frances
went to fetch Jamie from Lawson and laid him on a rug surrounded by
his adoring young aunts, who tickled him while he kicked his little legs
and gurgled with laughter. Watching Maria's soft eyes and gentle
touch, Frances thought she would make a good mother. At the right
time.

"Lady Braithwaite keeps a very… informal house," Lady Torridon
said to her fellow dowager. "She is very tolerant."

"It is her nature," Frances's mother said. "I own it was not my way, but I like it. It's good to have my children and grandchildren around me."

Frances smiled warmly at her mother. She had no idea if this seed would bear fruit, but she was happy to try. In the meantime, she felt something of Serena's excitement in going to Tamar Abbey. Frances now looked forward to returning to Torridon and making it truly into the home she and Alan wished it to be.

She told him something of this as she padded back to bed that night after laying Jamie down to sleep in his cradle.

"Of course," he replied at once, pulling back the covers and taking her straight into his arms. "We can change rooms around, redecorate, buy new furniture… the formal dining room always seems oppressive to me. And the drawing room."

"Oh, I'm so glad you said that! And we could entertain, invite friends more often, even hold a ball. We could invite particular friends to stay."

"Of course. It's time the place was livelier. Also… how would you feel about changing bedchambers? Mine is so distant from yours that it is positively isolating. It's as if we each have our own wing in the house!"

She hugged him. "I think that is an excellent idea."

"I thought we could turn my adjoining sitting room into your bedchamber. There are smaller rooms leading off both that we could make into private sitting rooms if we wished."

"I should like that," she said.

He caught the hem of her night rail, deliberately pushing it up and over her arms and head. His breathing quickened as his eyes devoured her in the candlelight. "Although I admit I have an ulterior motive. My aim, if you don't banish me, is to sleep in your bed every night."

Only when he said the words did she realize they were what she most wanted to hear. Her whole body flushed under his caresses.

"Just sleep?" she said breathlessly.

"Eventually," he said, cupping her full breasts, and softly kissing them. "I want to love you every night and every morning. And in between, I want to fall asleep with you in my arms. I had almost forgotten how beautiful you are…"

He rolled so that she lay on top of him. Her hair fell around them like a curtain, while they kissed. And then, for the first time, she explored his body as she had always longed to, inch by inch. Desire smoldered as she smoothed her palms over the hard planes and rippling muscles, kissing each battle scar, trailing her fingertips over his chest and downward to his waist and hips and thighs, to the erect shaft between.

In a surge of lust, wanton and daring, she took him within her. He groaned, holding her hips as though to savor the moment.

"Love me as you did this afternoon," she whispered.

"That was then," he said, "This is now, and different. We have all night."

And so he showed her the beauty of long, languorous loving. Unhurriedly, they took each other on a sensual, rambling journey that brought them each to joy. Several joys. Only then, totally and deliriously exhausted, did they fall asleep.

Chapter Eighteen

THE WONDER OF last night, and indeed all the events of the preceding day, were still with Frances as she fed Jamie the following morning. Alan slumbered on beside her, his face contented and boyish in sleep, his bandaged arm flung up on the pillow above his head. A fresh rush of love flooded her, for him and the baby in her arms.

How can one woman be so lucky? She smiled to herself because when she had left Torridon so recently, her emotions had been so different. Not the love. That had always been there, but it had not made her happy. She was wiser now.

With her free hand, she stroked her husband's hair off his forehead. From outside came the clip-clop of horses trotting up the drive to the front of the house. It must have been later than she had thought, although no one had disturbed them.

Since Jamie had stopped feeding to do a bit of gurgling and smiling instead, she slid out of bed and carried him to the window. Gillie and Lord Wickenden were dismounting as a groom ran up to take the horses. On impulse, Frances adjusted her nightgown to its proper state, and threw open the window.

"Good morning!" she called down. "Am I late, or are you early callers?"

"We're early," Gillie shouted back, waving. "Eager to share the news!"

"What news?" Frances asked.

"The war is over," Wickenden answered. "The Russians are in

Paris, and Bonaparte has abdicated. Finally!"

Abruptly, Torridon all but smacked into her back. Totally naked and using her as a shield, he called, "Truly?"

"Truly." Wickenden waved his newspaper. "The details are all here."

"We're coming down," Torridon assured him.

"Goodness," Frances said awed, as he closed the window. The war had been going on as long as she could remember—longer, in fact. "It seems everything is changing. A new dawn, a new life. There will be peace. At last."

Torridon took Jamie from her and placed him in the center of the bed, where he did his best to turn over. Frances laughed and threw herself into her husband's arms, spinning him around in a mad waltz.

"This is wonderful!" she exclaimed. "Such a year for everyone. And now the girls, Jamie, all our children will grow up with peace. I have such a good feeling about this next year, and the ones following, too! For all of us—Gervaise and Eleanor, Serena, Gillie, Kate, and our other friends."

"Yes, my love, the whole world is happy," Torridon said with tolerant amusement.

"Well, it should be," she insisted. "*I* am."

He kissed her. "I hope you always will be."

And she was.

Mary Lancaster's Newsletter

If you enjoyed *The Wicked Wife*, and would like to keep up with Mary's new releases and other book news, please sign up to Mary's mailing list to receive her occasional Newsletter.

http://eepurl.com/b4Xoif

Other Books by Mary Lancaster

VIENNA WALTZ (The Imperial Season, Book 1)

VIENNA WOODS (The Imperial Season, Book 2)

VIENNA DAWN (The Imperial Season, Book 3)

THE WICKED BARON (Blackhaven Brides, Book 1)

THE WICKED LADY (Blackhaven Brides, Book 2)

THE WICKED REBEL (Blackhaven Brides, Book 3)

THE WICKED HUSBAND (Blackhaven Brides, Book 4)

THE WICKED MARQUIS (Blackhaven Brides, Book 5)

THE WICKED GOVERNESS (Blackhaven Brides, Book 6)

THE WICKED SPY (Blackhaven Brides, Book 7)

THE WICKED GYPSY (Blackhaven Brides, Book 8)

REBEL OF ROSS

A PRINCE TO BE FEARED: the love story of Vlad Dracula

AN ENDLESS EXILE

A WORLD TO WIN

About Mary Lancaster

Mary Lancaster's first love was historical fiction. Her other passions include coffee, chocolate, red wine and black and white films – simultaneously where possible. She hates housework.

As a direct consequence of the first love, she studied history at St. Andrews University. She now writes full time at her seaside home in Scotland, which she shares with her husband, three children and a small, crazy dog.

Connect with Mary on-line:

Email Mary:
Mary@MaryLancaster.com

Website:
www.MaryLancaster.com

Newsletter sign-up:
http://eepurl.com/b4Xoif

Facebook Author Page:
facebook.com/MaryLancasterNovelist

Facebook Timeline:
facebook.com/mary.lancaster.1656

Manufactured by Amazon.ca
Bolton, ON

18829898R00122